Arthur Robins

Black Moss
A tale by a tarn. Vol. 2

ISBN/EAN: 9783337070540

Printed in Europe, USA, Canada, Australia, Japan

Cover: Foto ©Andreas Hilbeck / pixelio.de

More available books at **www.hansebooks.com**

Arthur Robins

Black Moss

A tale by a tarn. Vol. 2

BLACK MOSS.

A Tale by a Tarn.

BY THE AUTHOR OF

"MIRIAM MAY," AND "CRISPEN KEN."

IN TWO VOLUMES.

VOL. II.

LONDON:

RICHARD BENTLEY, NEW BURLINGTON STREET.

1864.

CONTENTS

OF

THE SECOND VOLUME.

BLACK MOSS.

CHAPTER I.

HOW GUY MELCHIOR REFUSED TO BE PREFERRED.

GIDEON CUYP, as he dipped along that afternoon behind that wall, had heard too much either for his ease or his peace. He had heard two things which were not pleasant to hear. He now knew that the Vicar of Black Moss conjectured that something might be wrong about the coat which had been carried to Job Redcar. Guy Melchior, it is true, told Minna that he wanted to be rid of the suspicion; but then he might not always so want to be rid of it. Therefore he had got this trouble from the journey he

made behind that wall.   And was there not
this other trouble also?   Had not the vicar
made a little speech, and told to Minna
Norman how hopelessly he loved her?   And
after the speech was so delivered did she
not rather fondly call him "Guy"?   And
then she had not screamed, or otherwise
pronounced against the liberty, when he had
kissed her.   These were such things as were
hard to be forgotten.   The sound of that
kiss was always in his ears, till, in the end,
he was horribly afraid that something would
be coming of it.   He did not think so much
about the coat, or the suspicion, which
sometimes sat so heavily upon the vicar.
No; he said to himself that in this matter
he did not fear what the clergyman could
do.   He did not believe in the sufficiency
of those proofs which might be brought
against him.   The rats were clever rats, but
they could not tell the story of their domes-
ticity; they could not tell how they got
back to the drain from whence they came.
So he no longer feared to be accused of the
rats.   And then the vicar did not know

about the changing of that bottle, or what
had been done to him when he lay there on
that bed in that saving perspiration. Cuyp
was sure that none had watched his going
in or coming out. So he was minded that
the bottle and the perspiration should not
further plague him. But then there was
that business of the coat—a business which,
if worked up, might have an awkward seeming. He knew there might be danger to
him in the story of that coat. All would
have been well if Job Redcar had but died.
But then Job Redcar lived, and was mending every day. Therefore Gideon Cuyp
could no longer conceal from himself that
the removal of Guy Melchior, for a variety
of causes, would be a desirable thing. Not
that he then bethought him of any removal
which would be one of violence. But he
would·like to see the · Vicar of Black Moss
preferred. Guy Melchior was too great a
clergyman for that valley. So excellent a
parish priest needed a more considerable
field. He might even rise to reach to many
and high dignities. This was the sort of

removal that Gideon Cuyp assured himself
that he desired for Guy Melchior, when
first those fears about the coat came gathering upon him.

Now the undertaker of Black Moss
reasoned within himself, that it would not
be hard to wipe out all traces of that night's
work which had been done by those half-
dozen home-sick rats. And after he had
so reasoned he went out and destroyed
them utterly. Neither did he conceive it to
be a hard thing to stay the blending of the
mountain-fed stream and the churchyard-
fed drain. Perhaps they had already
blended a little too long. And so before
another day had gone by he put away this
terror; and then, so far, he fancied his safety
to be very sure. There was only the coat
that could harm him now; and then the
thought of what that might do to him did
terribly disturb him. Sometimes he was
up about it, and sometimes he was down;
but he was oftenest down.

Gideon Cuyp, when so down, was always
full of the belief that Guy Melchior ought

to be preferred. The saintly life of the vicar was a beautiful thing for Black Moss to look upon; but then it was a great pity that only such a few could look upon it. At such moments the undertaker, who was not generally given to care about matters ecclesiastical, almost wished he was a bishop, that he might send up his friend. And yet he knew he did not love the vicar well. Even in those early days he was not sure but that if the vicar could not get preferred he must be otherwise got rid of. Gideon Cuyp would not have harmed his pastor, at least he thought so then. But the vicar must go; of that was he very sure. And when he came, after a little while, to be so sure of this, he knew he was not thinking pleasant or friendly things when he thought about Guy Melchior. As months went on, this which he felt the rather grew and mastered him; and as it followed him with spectral shape, he was sometimes nearly at his wits' end to get quit of its ghostly and terrible embraces. He was not the fearless man he used to be, full of his own strength, and

thinking to crush it. Now he had fallen
away to the weakness of believing he was
followed by a spectre, and was full of the
terror of being crushed. He would have
given a great deal—a great deal even of his
gold—had he not gone behind that wall.
He bethought him whether some of this
money he had gotten could not buy him
peace. No; he knew he must not offer to
the vicar anything to leave. But then
from whatever he started, he always did
come back to this—that Guy Melchior must
be got to go.

Gideon Cuyp had heard the words of the
vicar's weakness and falling away. He had
heard from behind that wall the wild avowal
of an awful love, which had broken from the
pauper-priest. He knew the vicar loved
her whom it was meant should be sold for a
high price—and now he almost feared that
there would be no sale. For he had seen
how Minna's heart had not been set on cal-
culating the barrenness of the vicar's yearly
incomings, or the emptiness of his purse.
No; she had not rebuked his words, and she

had not turned herself away from the taking of his kiss. He had seen her in the arms of the beggarly clergyman—and had not that been followed by the worse familiarity of a little hugging? His heart misgave him, that after such hugging there could come to be a sale. For all of which was the undertaker purposed that the vicar should not stay.

Gideon Cuyp had so played the eavesdropper to his great and his endless unrest. He did not believe that in the matter of loving Minna, Guy Melchior could go so far and no farther. He did not believe the vicar would presently think it enough to love the girl, as he would love a friend. He could not but think that it would end in his asking her to be his wife—to go home with him to nothing. He had heard Guy Melchior tell to her, he should never—because of his lack of means—ask of her to become his wife. But then, he did not believe that in coming to such resolutions it was given to men to be faithful. He believed that men only lied to themselves when they

said, that they could, after such a sort, be
strong.   If Guy Melchior loved, and was
loved, of Minna Norman, then Cuyp greatly
feared that they would come together.

He had not betrayed his uneasiness and
his troubles in this matter so far to Lady
D'Aeth.   It was his experience that clergymen did generally make fools of women;
and it occurred to him that even she might
find it to be worth her while to play him
false.   So was he tormented; and so he
went about seeking, with ill success, to shut
out the conviction that this was more than
a foolish fancy which had fastened on him.
In this manner many months went by.   He
did not hear that Minna had been asked
of any one to be his wife—therefore, on the
whole, the undertaker thought that things
were going ill.

Now there was just this from which he
got a little comfort.   Looking at all the circumstances, Gideon Cuyp was well and
steadfastly persuaded that Guy Melchior and
Minna Norman did not clandestinely cor-
respond.   He did not know whether, if he

could, he would have opened any of the letters, had they so corresponded. But he rather thought it would have been his business, as her guardian, to have done so. He came to the persuasion that, in this matter, there was nothing wrong in this way.

" Is there owt for th' vicar this mornin', Jacob?" he asked on one occasion, of Jacob Cringlemire, the old postman. " A's joost geean tae see him, an' a caan likely enoo' saave ye th' wark."*

But Jacob was not one of those who believed, as so many in these parts did, in the rectitude of Gideon Cuyp. Not only had the undertaker, to the mind of the postman, grievously overcharged a friend for a very plain elm shell; but, further than this, Jacob had heard the story of the coat from Job Redcar, when Job had once been confidential, thinking he should die. And although Jacob was no longer young, yet had he all his faculties; and he thought that if only half his faculties had still been

---

* **Walk.**

spared him, he could have seen with half an eye through Gideon Cuyp. He had noticed the writing on the letters which had come so steadily to the Vicarage; and he also knew from whom that writing came. But Jacob was too many for the undertaker, and did not mean to tell him any of the secrets of his bag. And in meaning this it is grievous to say that he lied to the undertaker.

"Nae, nae, Mr. Cuyp, nowt at awe er kind. I'll nit be trooblin' ye tae carry foma;* an' what's meear, I've nivver hed sae mooch es yan lettre tae drap there—let ma be thinkin' happen sen last back end. His friends, puir mon, don't sim tae be sae varra rank—they don't, hawivver." And then Jacob went his way to leave a letter for the vicar, which letter bore the London post-mark.

Now Gideon Cuyp might have known about these letters had he asked of the vicar if he ever heard from Minna; but then, as has been said, he went in fear of the Vicar of Black Moss. These letters were only about organ-players and Sunday-schools. Still, did

* For me.

he not know to what such writing, in such
cases, generally tended? Therefore Cuyp
was comforted by this picture of the Vicar's
loneliness and friendliness, as it had been
held up by the postman Jacob. And for a
time he was minded he would think no more
of that which he had heard behind the wall,
and which had so disquieted him. Nevertheless, the feeling that he was not very safe,
and that, perhaps, the Vicar might deliver
him up to make things clear about that
coat, would sometimes come upon him all
the stronger, and very terribly possess him.
And then he would take thought about the
getting rid of Guy.

It was in this mood that he one day got
a letter from Lady D'Aeth. It was a part of
the understanding that she should write and
tell him from time to time how it fared with
Minna, and this had been done. But as yet
she had not been able to tell Cuyp all that
he cared to hear, that Minna Norman was
going to be married to money. And this
letter which he had got now told him how
that she might have so married money, only
that she had declined the match.

It went on to tell him of their probable early return to Black Moss Abbey; it might be during the next week, certainly before the season was over; and it came to an end in these words :—" Remember us very kindly to the vicar. I think that our dear Minna will be very glad indeed to be back again— to get to the schools and the organ; for her heart, I am sure, is at Black Moss continually."

There was more than this, but then in every line it was only getting worse, and yet this was bad enough. "Her heart, I am sure, is at Black Moss continually:" this was more than her loving uncle could bear, although even he might be included in the things her heart went after. Why had he not gone into the world to sell this girl himself? Why had he left her sale in other hands? Yes, the organ and the schools—such had ever been the devices of those priests. And now he asked of himself with terrible meaning, " Why had he let this priest remain ?"

Gideon Cuyp crushed up the letter in his

hands, and flung it with an oath upon the floor. He dipped round and about it, and he cursed and he blasphemed. He had never believed much in the authority of clergy-men, but now he was very sure from whence they came. Never had even his hideousness looked nearly so hideous at any time before. Guy Melchior, then, *had* done this thing! What business had *her* heart to be in the keeping of so great a beggar? Now he saw it all. She had not been thinking of the vicar only as a friend; therefore the vicar should be *made* to go for the thing which he had done—the priestly fooling at the organ and the schools was ended.

After that Gideon Cuyp had purposed how Guy Melchior should be got away he picked up the letter, that by looking at what was written there again, he might the better see whether of a surety the words which had so moved him were not an illusion sent to plague him. So he picked the writing up, and then was very sure it had not been meant to mock him—for none of it was blotted out. It had the rather settled down, as it seemed to him, the clearer and the sharper on the pages. And now, what was worse, the words that had unstrung him had companions easy to be comprehended. There had been more than he had read before. So he carried the letter to the light, and there he saw that this was written :—

"I am afraid to say, the dear girl has, to my certain knowledge, declined several very eligible, unexceptionable offers. But no one seems to please her. She alone seems happy when we talk about Black Moss. She might have married a duke— she might have married an earl, yet she has decided to refuse them both. I never knew a girl so much admired. For the last six weeks all the fortunes in the land have followed her; and some have come to her who would, I think, have made her happy; but, perhaps, she knows best. I should, however, say that it was only last week she refused the richest baronet in England. He did not inquire what she had, or might expect to have; he would have married her, I am sure, if she had nothing. I thought

very highly of him, and was grieved at his
ill success ; the refusal, nevertheless, I have
reason to know was positive, and I do not
think he will return. She certainly threw
away an immense fortune, for he is almost
possessed of a county ; indeed, they do say
that he has a thousand a-day. Her dowry
would probably have not been less than half
a million of money. It could scarcely have
been below it. And then he had been so
excellently brought up ; I do not think he
has any of the vices so common to young
men. Indeed, I am sure that his principles
are beyond his years—but it seems she told
him that he must not even hope—and then
he is very handsome—I do not put much
value upon looks ; but this does make it all
the more difficult to understand why she
has refused him. With such a fortune, so
well-principled, and so well-looking, what
could she desire more ? But, as I have
said, it is clear she does not at all desire
him. Then, at the present, Mr. Massareene,
the most popular public man in England,
the heir to very large estates, is paying her

marked attentions. He follows her every-
where; and I have thought . it well he
should not be discouraged. It is not so
much that he will have an immense fortune, as that he has so many virtues. It
would delight me much to see our Minna
the wife of such a man as Mr. Massareene.
But, then, I can see that she is purposed to
answer him as she has answered all the rest,
and I do not believe that his addresses will
meet with any better success. She is so
sweet and gentle, that I almost fear to
question her lest she might think that I
was urging her; and though I regret her
judgment, I would not press her on these
matters for the world; and in so doing I
am sure that I am only carrying out your
wishes. Myself, I believe she does not
fancy she would like the sort of life these
marriages would bring her — something
quieter and humbler,- perhaps, would suit
her better. And she is such a darling, so.
good, so genuine, so lovely, that she ought
to have her own way. You will scarcely be
able to understand how much she has been

admired. And yet, with so many speaking to her of their love, she does not disguise that she would be rather back in 'dear Black Moss;' therefore I have concluded that she ought to come. Do you think her heart can have been touched before she left you? for I am almost inclined, sometimes, to think· that she must have some attachment that we do not know of.

"Believe me,

"Ever sincerely yours,

"SYDNEY D'AETH."

The crumpled letter fell from the hand of Gideon Cuyp when he had ended reading this. If there had been any more to read he could not have read it then; nor could he yet believe that he had now read it rightly. She would not be sold; he knew the letter told him this. Why had he kept her near and about him? Why had he been to her as a father? He limped to and fro his room. He was thinking of Guy Melchior when he so limped backwards and forwards. "She must have some attach-

ment that we do not know of." These
were the words that he could not shut out
of his ears when he bethought him of the
priest. But this priest was going; nothing
should stop his going now.

And then he picked up the writing and
read it again.

"He is almost possessed of a county.
They do say that he has a thousand pounds
a day. Her dowry would, probably, have
been half a million of money. It could
scarcely have been below it. His principles"—but then they had nothing to do
with the money which had been cast back in
his face. Could it be that it all was true?
Perhaps this was done that he might be
presently surprised. If he had not heard
those words of Guy's from behind that wall,
he might have thought this was a pleasantry.
But now he knew it was true. He knew
that Minna had given herself to that priest.
It was very awful indeed; it was more than
he could bear; at least he could not bear it
standing still. There was no hope left him
—but in the going that he had contrived for
Guy.

"Sick* a site ov brass, an' tae loss it awe.†
Hey mon, bet what a sad an' sorry marpie
I's bin," he gasped out as he took another
turn. "Tae kip her es I've kipt her, an'
nivver tae hoonger her.‡ I hev' had ivver
aboot me soomut that's sick a sticker; that'll
be likely tae be stoppin' olas omma § hends.
That'll be coomin' bock like a sorry shillin'.
Annudther attarchment! I's clean fashed; an'
hef a meellon a moony, a thousand poonds a
day; I isn't messel I knaa, I isn't when a
bethink ma aboot it. I's cleean capped.
It's awfool. I'll be doin' yon gae priest a
parlish meeschief. I weel, hawivver."

And then there was no longer left in him
the strength to cry or curse aloud. He
could only moan. He could only whimper,
and drivel, and pule. He could not take
another turn up and down his room, for the
power of his legs was gone. Only threats
of some crime he was working out could
come in bubbles to his lips. He had been
stricken so that he could not lift up his
head. He clutched at the air, colourless

* Such.　† All.　‡ Starves.　§ Always.

and ghastly, struggling like a child for words that would not fit his tongue. He could have borne to have heard of her dishonour if there had been a great price paid for her fall, for he would have been the richer by her shame. But this priest—what could he pay for setting her by his side as his lawful wife? Would God ever be giving to His servant more than one hundred pounds a year? And so did he froth on until, with a fearful laugh, he rolled heavily over with set and staring eyes, upon the floor.

When, after a little while, Gideon Cuyp came to, it instantly occurred to his ready and his rested mind, whether he had not altogether forgotten himself, whether it were not a peril and a weakness so to be overset upon the floor; and that it might be the better for his interests, if under such impulses and visitations, he should keep himself, if not composed, which was perhaps asking something too much, at any rate conscious, for when he had come to, the old woman who served his meals, and made his bed, was on her knees by his side throwing water on his face; having previously pro-

ceeded to tear from off him many of his
upper clothes. And then she might have read
the letter on the which he had fallen, which
letter would probably have accounted for
this temporary derangement of his faculties.
Therefore he shook her off, and dried himself, and put on again his upper clothes, and
got up on to his legs; and he next disposed
himself to the finding out if the old woman
could read. Grimly acknowledging her services with the water-pot, he smiled upon
her after his best manner—for he could
put himself through these changes with a
great speed—and then he said that perhaps
sometimes she might be feeling a little dull
at nights, and inquired of her whether or no
the loan of a Testament—which Minna had
given to him before she went away—might
be agreeable.

"Theanky, Mr. Cuyp, it's for ivver a
blessed booke, yu'd gimma;* a serious blessed
screeptur', an' a coomforatable, it is sooa,
bet I's no scholard at awe. I canna' reead,
an' noo I's a deal o'er aald tae discern th'
writin'."

* Give me.

And then she gathered up her water-pot, and got out, for she was afraid lest he might further question her.

Now Gideon Cuyp, on the whole, was assured that in this matter, the woman had not spoken falsely; and with this assurance he was not a little comforted. But then there was still the letter. The thousand a day, the half a million of money, which the girl had flung away. Something must be done to turn her mind aright, or these moneys would cease to be offered altogether. So he got him a little tea, for he was not yet fully fresh, and then he sent off this to Lady D'Aeth. The undertaker's writings were better than his conversations, as they often are with others of his class in Cumberland.

"HONOURED MADAM,

"Our dear Minna, as you say, is such a treasure to us both, that she oughtn't to be urged. But I think it's rather a pity that the half million of money shouldn't have come into the family. The Baronet, with the high *principles* and the thousand a day, and that half a million of money, wouldn't have been amiss. I know I don't set so much on the brass as some do; but still it's a pity that Minna didn't think more about his high *principles*. These are the things I want to see in the man who marries our girl. Although of course a little money wouldn't be objectionable; only Minna must know best."

Gideon Cuyp, when he came to this, sat back in his chair, and took a look at his work. He put in the stops, and a thick line under "principles," and then he thought that, as far as it went, it could not be mended. But that which he had now to do would have to be done in quite his best manner; for this business was to be about Guy Melchior, and if he was to set his hand to anything that was not well, it might go hardly with him by-and-bye. So he sat up again and after this sort lied :—

" The vicar wants me to say that Minna's young friends are very badly wishing to get her back, and that the organ hasn't seemed

to be right somehow since she went away ;
and it certainly do make very strange
noises. He is a worthy man, honoured
madam, this vicar of ours; a regular soldier
of Christ, and no mistake; and I say he is
too good for the ranks, and ought to get sent
up higher. It seems hard that he isn't
better to do than he is. I often thinks to
myself that it's very much against him his
stopping here. He's wasted like, as I say,
in such a poor spot. Couldn't this Mr.
Massareene, this great minister, do something for him? About the half a million,
and the high principles; if the gentleman
was to come again,—I don't want to press
on Minna,—but I think it wouldn't be amiss
if she closed with him; there isn't such a
sight of principle about in these days.

"I am, honoured Madam,
"Very respectfully yours,
"GIDEON CUYP."

Now Cuyp had thought that he would add
to this something about the "attachment"
with the vicar; but if it so chanced that

any harm should befall Guy at any time,
something that would not be well might
come of it; therefore he decided that he
would not add it. And then, besides, if that
letter did not rid him of the priest, why the
getting rid might perhaps be otherwise
accomplished. So he put on it his seal and
let it go.˙

Gideon Cuyp had, however, taken much
counsel of himself before he could be at all
persuaded that this flourish which he had
flourished would do his work—before he
could persuade himself that it concealed and
revealed enough. One passage there was
that seemed to him to be extraordinarily
fine—" the soldier of Christ not getting up
out of the ranks"—pleased him mightily.
Therefore, as has been said, he concluded
that it met every difficulty and challenged
every contingency, and so let it go.

When this very cautious and well considered writing got into the hands of Lady
D'Aeth was on that morning which followed
the great ball at Windermere House—that
is, on the morrow of that night on the which

Minna Norman, in that corridor, had had that question put to her by the Privy Councillor, and had answered in so few words that she could " never love him." Therefore in this matter the mischief was done whilst Cuyp's letter was yet on its way. But then Lady D'Aeth did not at all know that this mischief had been done. So she was not long in resolving what she would do. She had not seen that there was anything between Minna and the vicar other than a general tendency in Minna to the liking of spiritual things—a tendency common to her sex and years. Lady D'Aeth did not mean that Minna should marry where she could not freely give her heart. But then she had never bethought her that Minna would care to marry ever with a curate who had only one hundred pounds a year, and had his home in a swamp in Black Moss. She knew that clergymen sometimes did offer themselves to young girls with money ; but she had not known of young girls with money losing themselves to unfashionable clergymen in outlying places.

She meant that Minna should presently have a great deal of money; nevertheless she did not see with whom Minna would best like to share it. So the great letter of Gideon Cuyp did in no wise open her eyes.

Lady D'Aeth, with all her singleness of heart, was now minded warmly to befriend the cause of Guy Melchior by bringing his claims, as a faithful and good man, before the favourite minister; and having answered Cuyp's letter, she proceeded also to address a petition to Fabian Massareene. Had she known of the question and the answer in that corridor, where Minna and the minister were cooling themselves, it may be assumed that she would not now so have addressed the minister.

It was a little after noon when a note was put into the hands of Fabian Massareene. It brought to his favourable notice one Guy Melchior, a vicar in a Cumberland valley, at present in the lawful receipt of one hundred pounds a year; and it further pleaded for the preferment of this clergyman, setting forth his qualities and his virtues in terms that were not to be mistaken.

The minister, when he put this down, thought that he read more than in that letter was written. He thought he could see why there was some grave doubt as to who should wear the Massareene gems. He knew that a poor clergyman could generally hold his own amongst the richest of lay sinners; and he doubted not but that one of the qualities of this estimable young priest was, that he had been able to recommend himself to Miss Minna Norman. Now Massareene thought only very indifferently of clergymen, but he also knew what was their strength with womankind.

A motive for calling in S. James's Place that had been all that morning trying to assert itself, would now, he conceived, be satisfied by his replying to this petition in person; and after no very lengthened survey of the situation, he resolved to present himself that afternoon to Lady D'Aeth. He did not believe that Lady D'Aeth had heard of that which had passed between Minna and himself.. She could not have asked this of him if she had; and then, if he were to bring himself to ask anything again of Minna Norman, it would be as well, perhaps, that Lady D'Aeth should be his friend. It was very necessary that something should be done; for his father had again written to him concerning an heir, and his mother worried him about the diamonds. So he was resolved that he would go to S. James's Place that afternoon.

The pride of Fabian Massareene had surely been lately setting some snares for him. He had long believed, with a very full belief, that he had only to show himself to be followed of women; that he had only to ask and to have; and latterly he had become so possessed with this conceit, that before he had so offered himself to Minna Norman, he had written to his mother to say that such of the gems as were in old-fashioned setting must be at once reset, because that he was immediately going to settle; and he also wrote to his father to announce that he had found one who would

be a becoming mother for his heir. There-
ore, seeing that this writing had gone forth
to the old people in Yorkshire, it was awkward and embarrassing that Minna should
so have answered him the night before.
He would be getting their congratulations
by the next post, and it might be that
the diamonds were already on the way
to Bond Street. So he now felt that he
must get this girl. If she could not give to
him her love, yet must he have her without
it. The whole Riding might be already
talking of his nuptials; there was no
reckoning the ridicule that would come upon
him if the Riding were.

As has been seen, it had not, at any time,
entered into the mind of Fabian Massareene
to conceal the possibility of his not being
eagerly appropriated by any woman; and,
therefore, the answer of Minna Norman had
set him seriously conjecturing how he might
overcome the catastrophe which had come
upon him outside that ice-room ; how, indeed, he might, perhaps, change the manner
of his suit, and gain his ends. He might

seem to befriend this needy vicar, and he might yet be contrivnig his undoing. Indeed, this letter of Lady D'Aeth did almost seem like an invitation to get rid of this sorry priest. But he would go and see how the ground did lie.

When Fabian Massareene had mastered this letter which he had got from Lady D'Aeth, he was at once well assured that Minna Norman had not anywhere disclosed his discomfiture, or she would first have told her aunt. Through all the hours of the morning, indeed ever since he got her answer, he had come to the resolve, at all risks, to carry his point, and make Minna Norman his wife, or the whole county would presently be ringing with ridicule. It was not even impossible that his mother might now be bearing about the news. It was very terrible that he who had warned all men might now make them to laugh. It was terrible to him to think that there might be those who were already canvassing the qualities of mind and person of his selected bride—the bride of his choice, who in her turn, had contumaciously refused to be so chosen. How great a fool had he been to write about his heir and the diamonds as he so had written! This was what he thought about himself all that morning through. The woman he had resolved should be the mother of his heir, was shrinking from the honour of wearing the diamonds, or of lengthening his line. Why had he thought so highly of himself? Why had he given this occasion to all men to scoff? There was no escape from this scoffing if he could not have her; therefore he cursed and called himself a fool.

And then, he bethought him, these things very early get to spread, and in a week or less it might come to be told, with appropriate caracaturing, even in every club in London, that he, Fabian Massereene—that he, the favourite and omnipotent minister, in his great condescension at the last to take a wife, himself had not been taken. And because of this he knew that he had been a very fool.

Therefore, come what might, he felt he

must get Minna. So when the afternoon
was growing on, he sent up his name in
S. James's Place. He caused it to be believed there that he was just on his way
to the House, and had only a few minutes
for such light things as were the preferment of obscure vicars, that he could spare
from the graver things of the nation. But
then, he also caused it to be seen that these
few minutes were very heartily at the service
of Lady D'Aeth.

Fabian Massareene, when he had
mounted those stairs, and had got into the
room, had never perhaps been more gay,
more fluent, more worthy of the name for
high and easy bearing, that he had gotten;
and never less embarrassed and forced.
With consummate delicacy he left it to Lady
D'Aeth to say how the meritorious vicar
could best be served. And he did it all with
so much heartiness, that it seemed to the
lady as if the chief concerns of his mind
were the meritorious clergy. And yet was
he not too emphatic: in these things Fabian
Massareene always did preserve the mean.

" And now, Lady D'Aeth, may I ask who is this Mr. Melchior—this deserving and favoured priest, who has so succeeded in securing your sympathy?"

" Oh ! Mr. Massareene, did you not know that he is a very old friend of mine, and of Miss Norman's ? She helps at his schools, plays his organ, and is very busy in his blanket-club. You could not prefer a more deserving man than the Vicar of Black Moss."

Now, when Fabian Massareene heard these words about the schools, and the organ, and the blanket-club, he knew he had concluded that which was right in this matter. He knew that the loves of clergymen always did have these beginnings. He had hoped he might have concluded wrongly. But now that he had heard these things he was scarcely so sure that she would wear the diamonds. If Lady D'Aeth had told to him this priest's history she could not, whatever she might have said, have told to him more than he had gathered from the words she now had spoken. He was petitioned to prefer his successful rival ! But

yet he was calm and unruffled, and looked
to be very glad that he had been drawn in
to succour this priest!

"I will certainly at once speak to the
Archbishop, and will mention such conspicuous claims to the Lord Chancellor—
nor will. I forget to bring them before the
Premier: be assured so worthy a man shall
no longer be passed over." And after he
had said this, with a touch of sarcasm that
was very nicely veiled, he was let out, and
went his way to Westminster.

When the House broke up that night
Fabian Massareene at once addressed himself to the Premier, and then championed,
with more of warmth and earnestness than
was usual with him, the claims of Guy
Melchior. For did he not know that that
which he had to do must be done quickly?
It has been explained that the Premier was
only chief because for family reasons it was
a necessity that the Whig structure should
be raised on him; therefore Massareene
asked this of him, meaning that the Premier should do as he was bidden.

" Your young friend, Massareene, has, at any rate, not left his case to an indifferent advocate," said the chief of the families, smiling ; " but there is nothing, I think, at this moment—eh, is there ?—of course you know best. Stay, though—there *is* Sierra Leone ; only that's not quite the place to send a friend to—eh, Massareene ?"

Now, Massareene certainly thought otherwise. Such a friend as was his would be excellently well suited at Sierra Leone. No one could say that he wanted the young man's life ; but then the young man's life would be taken. So he concealed his feelings, and made this very judicious answer to his chief.

" Well—yes, of course there *is* danger ; but then this man, as I am told, likes dangers ; he courts them ; he seeks them ; he would do anything for the Gospel——"

" There are many of these men who will do anything for the Gospel, Massareene, who wont go out to Sierra Leone."

" That's very true ; but my friend's passion for fever is an enthusiasm."

"Then I should say that coast would not be likely to disappoint him. It may be his if he will have it, for has it not been going the round of even clerical destitution for a month or more?"

"Then I will offer it in your name." For it was not permitted to be seen of men that the chief of the Cabinet was other than at its head. And after this had been agreed, they parted.

Early the next day Fabian Massareene again presented himself at Lady D'Aeth's. He was authorized to say that the Prime Minister, in consideration of the distinguished parochial services of Mr. Melchior, would be pleased to recommend him for the vacant bishopric of Sierra Leone. "It is perhaps rather far, but you know it generally leads to something higher."

Now, of course Fabian Massareene by this might have meant that it generally led immediately to Heaven. But Lady D'Aeth was thinking, the rather, of temporalities, than of Guy Melchior being swept away by yellow fever. So when she heard of what was pro-

mised, she was very glad, and sent for Minna
Norman to tell to her the glad tidings. And
Minna heard how it was proposed to send
away the vicar, and was not glad at all.

"Thank you, Mr. Massareene; thank
you for your good offices," said Lady D'Aeth,
warmly; "this will be great news to our
poor vicar."

"But, aunt," put in Minna, sorrowfully
and wistfully, "it's so far to send him, and
he'll never come back. Sierra Leone, you
know, is in Africa; and if Guy—I mean, if
Mr. Melchior—should go there, I'm sure we
shall never see him again; and *you* wouldn't
like that, aunt, would you?"

"Our wishes, my love, must not be suffered to stand in the way of Mr. Melchior's
interest." And then she turned to the
minister and thanked him again for the
great glory that was to fall on Guy. After
which the minister went out, for he wanted
air.

Yes; now he knew everything; he had
heard her stumble with her tongue and call
him "Guy." It was very hard for the

proud man to feel that he was beaten by
this priest—by this one who could not always have meat set before him when he sat
him down to dine. Even if this priest was
got amongst the fever, the pride of the
favourite would none the less have had a
fall. But if the vicar *would* not go ? And
when he thought of that, the imaginings of
the minister were only vile.

The next day's post brought to Guy Melchior the offer in official terms. And in the
same night's ministerial paper, this was
caused to be announced: "We are in a
position to state that the vacant Bishopric
of Sierra Leone has been offered to the Rev.
Guy Melchior, of University College, Ox-
ford, and Vicar of Black Moss, Cumberland.
Mr. Melchior has been for many years an
indefatigable parish priest, and we believe
that this selection will command the ap-
proval of all parties in the Church."

Now this was putting upon the thing a
very proper glow ; and people who read it
said how well it was to have a Whig
Government, if only to get these good ap-

pointments. Public opinion, it is certain, had been very judiciously and wisely ordered and directed in this matter; for Fabian Massareene himself caused to be published this lying commentary on Government disinterestedness and Cabinet virtues. It was really quite a pity that the smoothness of this contriving did not last a little longer.

That morning the Vicar of Black Moss had appeared to the undertaker whilst he sat at breakfast, and Cuyp's greeting was, on the whole, perhaps a little confused. He did not know but that Guy might have come about the coat.

"No, no. Don't let me interrupt you; pray don't move. I have been offered preferment, Mr. Cuyp—the Bishopric of Sierra Leone——"

"Hey, mon, bet I's reet glaad, Mr. Melchior."

"And—and—I have concluded to decline it."

CHAPTER II.

CONCERNING SOME COUNSEL OFFERED TO THE
STATESMAN BY THE UNDERTAKER.

THE unprotected and helpless position of a
moribund Cabinet had that year demanded
a very early prorogation. The administration, indeed, had known that they could carry
nothing; therefore, ever since the first week
in February, they had done the bidding of
the opposition. The name of Fabian Massareene alone had kept them in their places;
so it was expedient that Parliament should
not be hanging on. That want of confidence, which was at last being undisguisedly
proclaimed throughout the country, might
have come at any time to take the form of
a vote of dismissal. And a vote of dismissal just then would have been very

inconvenient to the Government; for, in many directions, some patronage, not nearly contemptible, was shortly expected to accrue to the administration. There were two prelates being only kept alive by the prayers of the faithful, and by certain cordials; but no one believed that they could last until Parliament should again assemble. And then a puisne judge had got gout in his stomach. So it became very necessary that the spectacle of a helpless and an abject Government should be preserved until the beginning of another session. And the spectacle was accordingly preserved. By the last week in July the fish dinner was ordered and eaten, and the ministers were safe except from their own prodigious weakness. Still the Whig edifice, on the whole, seemed to be enduringly set up, for in its building none of the families had been rejected—so a very bad defeat or two was taken by the Government with great good humour, until at the last it came to be asked if anything would move them. And then the weather got to be very hot indeed, and members went after other business, and so it came to be that ministers were not disturbed.

Fabian Massareene, upon whose individual personal popularity, as has been said, his colleagues condescended to trade, turned himself away for once from the slaughtering of grouse and went down to Black Moss Abbey, on the invitation of Lady D'Aeth. Now Lady D'Aeth, who in this matter had not seen things very clearly, was still minded that Fabian Massareene should not be discouraged. But the minister had as yet said nothing to her—nor had Minna told her aunt about the question that had been asked in the corridor; therefore Lady D'Aeth thought to herself that nothing as yet had been spoken between them ; but as she thought it well that something should be spoken, the minister was asked to Black Moss Abbey as a friend, to speak if he so chose. Minna Norman did not think that so great a man as Massareene would ask that question of her any more ; otherwise she would have told her aunt of all that had

been done. After many days she knew it
would have been much better if she had.
So when she heard about his coming, she
said nothing; and from her silence, Lady
D'Aeth concluded that Minna would be
Mrs. Massareene.

Fabian Massareene, the while, had reasoned
much within himself, and concluded that
perhaps, upon the whole, it would not be
expedient to tell his father or his mother
that there was any such awkward obstacle
to his getting at once married, as his having
been unconditionally declined. It would
suffice if he desired that they would as
yet be silent concerning it; for since that
night when she had taken away his hand,
and had answered him so calmly, but so
firmly, he had been gradually getting to
be on better terms with himself again; and
now those terms were very good and flat-
tering; and he was presently persuaded
that she would yet have him gladly. Nor
had he, in this matter, even taken his mother
into any closer confidence. He had not told
her, who loved him with so great a love,

about his fall. There are those men, in all conditions, who never cease to hold themselves apart from any but the most reserved and imperfect communion with their father, who, nevertheless, do not and cannot refuse to lay the many burdens of their hearts before their mother, with only faith in her sweet sympathy, and without one fear of her reproaches. Let but a tear of hers fall upon the story of our sorrows, and we can bear and suffer patiently, for that alone has made our trouble soft, and given to us men the strength to stand. And the mother of this man had been very loyal and true to him. As he had been raised up, so had her joy gone with him—so had her pride been mounting— but her love and her pride would mount for all that he had fallen before the answer of this girl. And yet he turned himself away, and would not hear her comfortable words.

The outworks of the inner life of Fabian Massareene had never been passed, even by his mother, at any time from his youth up

until now. Even when he sat upon her
knee, and she would cry aloud for the great
love she bore him, she knew that she could
never set aside the challenge that always
met her at the outpost of suspicion. She
had heard how the master at Harrow ex-
horted the school to keep the example of
her boy before their eyes. She had heard
how the Master of Trinity had taken this,
her only son, by the hand, and said that
Cambridge was very proud of his success. She
had lived to see him later rising very high in
honour and in power. It had been explained
to her that only because the great Whig
families would have it so, was Fabian shut
out from being the corner-stone of the
Whig edifice; but that the next corner-
stone would be assuredly her son. Nevertheless, other than this, she had been permitted to know very little more about the
incidents and circumstances of his progress
than did the outer and the public world.
That he was now going to "settle," and
put her gems on some fair neck, was a great
deal more to her than his having become,

with so much success and haste, a Privy
Councillor ; and scarcely could the venerable
lady bear herself for joy. She had reached
to this length of days almost without one
hope of her life that was not fulfilled.
And now that her eyes were getting to be
dim, she yet would see this glory which was
come upon her son. And after this there
would be nothing left her mother's heart to
desire more, but yet a little further yield of
time to see and bless her boy's first-born;
and then she went out amongst her friends
and her neighbours, and took her husband,
who was very feeble, with her.

"I dare say it's quite right, my dear, for
it's quite time that Fabian should be thinking of an heir—but he didn't tell us, did he,
that we were to talk about it?" asked the old
gentleman, as he was lifted up into the
carriage. And then he sank back and left
it all to his wife to do as she thought
best.

"Why, it's not going to be a secret
marriage—everybody will be glad to hear
about it — and I am sure they ought to

know." And the old gentleman said he thought so too ; and so the coachman was ordered to drive on.

Fabian's mother, therefore, knew it would have been better if the coachman had not been so ordered to drive on, when she got that letter from her son, in the which he said that as the thing was not yet fully settled, nothing must be said about it. And then the old gentleman got up from his arm-chair and kissed her. "Never mind, my dear, it was all my fault—wasn't it, eh?—well, it wasn't yours." And then, having so comforted her, he crept back. He was four-score years and four ; and for fifty of those years he had been the true husband of that wife. After which that venerable lady wrote to her son, and told him how she had driven about to her friends and neighbours, and how she greatly feared that all the Riding now knew what he had done. And it must be said that Fabian answered her angrily and roughly, and told her it was not well that at her age she could not stay at home, or bear herself with more discretion

when she went abroad. And she confessed
that he reproved her rightly — for was he
not her very son, who could do nothing
wrong? Then she wrote to him very
humbly, and said that for the rest of her
time here she *would* bear herself with more
discretion when she went abroad. And
then, too, she would send to him more
letters than it pleased him to receive,
bidding him to urge his marriage on.
" When was he going to bring her whom he
loved to Massareene Court? When was
their new daughter to come to them to hear
the words of welcome that had been so long
laid up, so long unpronounced? For I so
yearn to see her, Fabian—and it must be
soon, or I and your father will be gone. She
who has given to you, my son, her love, of a
surety may reckon steadfastly upon your
mother's. I hear that many asked her; and
how I shall prize her that she sent them all
away for you. Should I ask this Lady
D'Aeth to come to Massareene Court? I
will do everything you tell me, Fabian. Or,
if I may not see this sweet girl, yet tell me

that I at least may write to her. I hear
that she is very beautiful and good—and
ought she not to be, to marry you? The
diamonds are nearly ready."

Now this was very inconvenient writing
for Fabian Massareene to get. He was fond
of his mother—in his way—but it seemed to
him that in this matter she took too much
upon herself. There was no saying what
harm might come of her having published
it over the Riding. Of course she was
not to ask Lady D'Aeth to Massareene
Court. And of course she was not to write
to Minna. It was very irritating and un-
pleasant to be asked these questions; but
then the irritation told him this—that it
was expedient he should persuade Minna
Norman to give to him at once a different
answer. That which was spoken in the
Riding would be presently the talk of England. He was very sure she would be his;
but then, as yet, these congratulations of his
mother were a little out of season. Therefore he disposed himself to the quieting
of her enthusiasm, and to the answering of

such of her questions as were not convenient with much address, and more equivocation.

These proofs of his mother's unabated and continuing interest in all that concerned him—in themselves but a weariness, for he was too selfish to see their unselfishness—however, did set before him a warning that he was not slow to turn to the best account. He became each day the better assured it was never ordered that he should be rejected by a woman. And so he became the more convinced that Minna Norman must be got to speak the words he wanted her to say, and their marriage hurried on. She must wear those diamonds, and she must give to him an heir ; but anyhow it must not be told before the world that he desired, and did not have—that she would not put the brilliants on, and shrank from the high destiny of giving him a son. So he decided he would go to Black Moss Abbey, and he went there so soon as Parliament was up, without first turning aside to visit his own home.

Fabian Massareene was yet of opinion that
Minna Norman had hitherto kept closely
the secret of that which was between them ;
and he thought that, on the whole, it was
better he should not at present speak to
Lady D'Aeth about it. He was sure she
was friendly, and that if she interfered, it
would be to tell Minna to do what was
right towards him. And then it would be
well that he should get to see this vicar
who so refused to be preferred. Guy Melchior must be sent out of Black Moss even
if preferment were not at the end of his
going. He did not fear this inconsiderable
priest. No ; Massareene was very sure he
had not fallen from his great height to such
a fear as that.

So little was he accustomed to be answered
other than as he pleased, and so abundantly
well was he satisfied that, even with Guy
Melchior on the spot proclaiming his one
hundred pounds a year, Minna Norman
would reconsider her decision, that, in the
end, he never doubted but that its reversal
would be ultimately secured. And in this

belief he went upon his way to Cumberland.

Now it was very true that Minna Norman
had not, so far, seen fit to tell to any one, not
even to her aunt, the nature and urgency
of Massareene's overtures, and her very
plain and summary rejection of them. She
did not believe that such an one as was he
would, because of the pride that was in him,
ask for her love again. So she concluded to
tell no one of it. But then she also resolved
how she would make answer if so be that
he should come to her again. Nor did she
so much shrink from his being at the Abbey,
because her heart was now lighter about
other things—was full of hopes and thoughts
that might not, it is likely, have been as-
suring to Massareene, had she taken to
publicly setting them out. She went to the
schools, and she took the organ, and she
had been received back as the head of the
blanket-club, and her heart was in her work;
and there, of course, as must needs be so, was
very often the vicar.

The marked attentions of the minister to

Minna Norman had been considered, by the
proper judges of these things, in all their
bearings, even by many ripe and practised
meddlers, throughout the season—from the
first May drawing-room, down to Lady Windermere's ball; and it was very generally concluded by these authorities that, in his present
mood, he meant to marry her. It was not
by any of these supposed that there could
be any reasonable doubt about anything
other than *his* intentions. He would certainly do as it might please him. She
might, they said, go through some of the
tricks of coyness, and be otherwise a
little artful; but her mock innocence would
not prevail against her having him. So
magnificent and much-sought a person as
was the minister need not busy himself with
such common considerations as might be
centred in the possibility of his getting his
dismissal out of the mouth of any woman.
It was not in the very least possible; therefore,
of course such great judges did not trouble
themselves further to consider it. When,
however, Fabian Massareene so quickly fol-

lowed Minna into the country, there was no longer any hesitation in the general belief that he fixedly purposed making her his wife.

Now Lady D'Acth had also got to be very sure that the minister did so fixedly purpose · to ask for the hand of Minna Norman. She did not see that Minna was concerned about the schools, or the organ-playing, because the vicar was more to her than her parish priest. Guy Melchior, ever since that day when in his great weakness he let fall those words which told to Minna of his love, had been outwardly to her only as he was before that day. He knew that she loved him and none other, and that because of his speaking she had thrown away so many men and so much money. He knew that he had stumbled terribly— badly as a man—but terribly as a clergyman. He knew that with one hundred pounds a year he should for ever have held his peace. And now he knew that another had come to carry her away. It would be very hard to look at this carrying away. It would be also very hard if she sent back Massareene, and very hard to feel that she had given her love to him who might not have it. Therefore Guy Melchior refrained himself from any other burning words, and now bore himself as should a sober clergyman ; so soberly that Lady D'Aeth was sure that he and Minna were not drawn closely to each other.

Then after a little while, it was stated in a courtly morning paper, that " the Right Honourable Fabian Massareene, M.P., has left town for Black Moss Abbey, Cumberland, the seat of Lady D'Aeth. The Right Honourable gentleman remains on a visit."

This supplied matter capable of much enlargement and improvement in an early number of a Cumberland paper. " The Right Honourable Fabian Massareene, M.P., has, we have reason to believe, arrived at Black Moss Abbey formally to propose for the hand of Miss Norman, whose remarkable personal attractions have throughout the past season created so marked a sensation in the highest circles."

This delicately conveyed announcement

was not, however, so made public until the
minister's stay at the Abbey had been pro-
longed over the first week, and he, meanwhile, had been performing cautiously on
Gideon Cuyp.

On the third day after Massareene's arrival
at Black Moss Abbey, Lady D'Aeth had
inquired of him how far it would be agreeable
to have brought before him Minna's uncle,
for in those days the minister did not seek
to conceal that he was much interested in
all concerning Minna Norman. Lady D'Aeth
had her hopes that the marriage might be
made. She would have desired it for Undine,
and now she desired it for Minna ; but she
was not going to hide away the undertaker
until Massareene and his bride should be
leaving the church. If Massareene meant
well and truly, he would not change his
mind because of Gideon Cuyp. She would
do this, though it might send the minister
away. And when she thought of this she
knew how much her heart was set on marrying Minna to this famous minister. It was
not altogether because of his brilliancy, or

his possessions, or his position, as she had written to Cuyp, that she so desired it. She believed him to have led an unblemished, and, at least, not a self-indulgent and licentious life; and that amongst many temptations to be irreligious and irregular, he had not fallen away. She had asked him to visit at the Abbey, not only because she wished him, in the course of events, to become the husband of Minna Norman, but that he might also have an opportunity of seeing something of Gideon Cuyp. And now that the minister was in her house— now that she saw him in that quiet place, and could better taste him than in London— now was she very sure that Fabian Massareene was even worthy of this gentle, peerless girl. But he must not tell Minna of his love, if it was his purpose so to tell her, till he had seen the undertaker. The blood of the coffin-maker did not show in Minna's veins. She was none the less a queen of girls for all that Cuyp might be. No; of this she was resolved, that if it pleased the minister he and the undertaker should meet at once.

Fabian Massareene was staying at the
Abbey only as the friend of Lady D'Aeth,
and not because it was intended to throw
Minna Norman at him; and although Lady
D'Aeth, on her part, was prepared to give
encouragement to the minister if he were
minded to ask for it, yet in no way did she
mean to urge Minna to yield an unwilling
consent even to this man. After he had
looked on Cuyp he might win her if he
could, but Minna only should determine how
he should be answered. Therefore this
talking about Minna never went beyond
the interest they mutually took in one so
beautiful and so much prized.

Fabian Massareene had, indeed, heard
something of the ugly calling of Gideon Cuyp
—that, he had thought, was not very pleasant
to hear. But then he had considered this
connexion, and thought that he could bear
it. Not even was the unlovely trade of a
maker of coffins going to stand in his way.
As he then felt, had he heard how Minna
used to do the pinking for the superior shells,
he was sure he would not have minded it.

And so this was the manner of his answering
to Lady D'Aeth :

"I have heard this much, my dear lady,
of Mr. Cuyp, that it rather makes me wish
to know more.   Miss Norman is enthusiastic
about his many and modest virtues.   His
coffins apart, he must be quite a character."

"Mr. Cuyp," said Lady D'Aeth, "is
unquestionably a very worthy man.   He
has been for years a great benefactor to these
parts. He is so simple minded, and generous,
and unassuming, that, hereabouts, it is not
too much to say he is widely loved.   It is
not a little, I can assure you, that the people
esteem him.   Indeed, I may tell you, speak-·
ing for myself, his active benevolence, his
kindliness, and his many charities almost
make one forget the hideousness of his
occupation."   And then Lady D'Aeth paused
a little before the revelation that she had
to make come out.   "You are probably
unaware, Mr. Massareene, that in this very
lonely valley we are not ignorant of this,
that our undertaker is, in his way, a distinguished and learned man.   Mr. Cuyp,

let me tell you, who is neither a quack nor an empiric, is the discoverer of a great invention—of an infallible powder for the preservation of the dead;" and Lady D'Aeth declared the service of Cuyp almost in a whisper, for that brought back memories which yet bore her down. And then she waited to see with what success she had so sounded the praises of the undertaker.

"Truly, my dear Lady D'Aeth, an original mind can almost cover even the ghastliness of an unpopular trade. The preservation of the dead ought to be to me, I suppose, just now a matter of some importance and of more anxiety. For do not they say of her Majesty's Government that we are a dead body?" And the minister who was not one of the departed, if he were one of the dead, smiled at his own pleasantry, after which he went on :—" Therefore, perhaps, Mr. Cuyp's incomparable powder may be as serviceable to a lifeless Cabinet as to a corpse. I should of all things like to see this chief of the undertakers. Pray let me make the introduction upon the earliest occasion."

"I am afraid you will be setting your expectations too high, Mr. Massareene, for he does not *look* to be the man he is. You would never take him for the uncle of my Minna."

The earliest occasion was that same evening after dinner. Gideon Cuyp had had a little note from Lady D'Aeth, asking him to come up to the Abbey. Therefore he put on his best suit—the suit he put on when he went in front of first-class funerals, and he tied about his throat a very stiff white tie of immense proportions—then, when this was done, he gathered up his best black gloves, and carried them up to the Abbey, but he did not put them on. He got to the outer door just before Lady D'Aeth and Minna were leaving for the drawing-room; and therefore, when he came into the room he bowed very low to the lady of the house, and was kissed by Minna, after which he shuffled up to the minister to make obeisance, and was sat down in front of the port wine.

"It's gae hot," he said, putting away his

damp gloves, and struggling to loosen his great tie; "bet I wont soop,* I wont soop owt for wine dae meeak ma breeak oot terble."† And he pushed away the port, and mopped his face with his pocket-handkerchief.

Then the ladies went away upstairs, and Massareene and the undertaker drew closer together. The minister had thought it would not be nice to have relations with this warm man, but he thought he would notwithstanding go on with that which he had set himself to do.

" It won't hurt you, this wine, Mr. Cuyp. Let me just persuade you to take one glass."

" Nae, nae, bet I'll hev nowt ta dae w'it. It's raank er fire, a knaa it is. A lile tinny soop fetches ma oot in drops awe o'er."

" Then I won't press you, Mr. Cuyp, if the effect is to make you so uncomfortable. And now let me say I am greatly interested in all I hear about this wonderful protective powder that your genius has discovered— probably its costliness alone prevents its being very widely used."

* Drink. † Terribly.

Now Cuyp did not quite know how to answer to this. Had the minister lost a friend, and was this the beginning of a bargain? It would not do to scare him away because of its costliness, neither would it do to let him have it too cheap. So he made a little speech that he thought would neither frighten away a purchaser, nor depreciate the article.

"There is a goode few pooders, awe oop an' down, a tak' it," said Cuyp, contemptuously, "bet they is awe baad alike. It's only mi ain that isn't a fraud. Mi charges, as it's goode to discern in this paper, sootes awe kind a fooak, bet then th' resoolt isn't purrishable. Girt families can die doon for a varra lile. Ten per cent. a draps off for th' first feeve, an' twenty-feeve per cent. for ivver eftre.* I hev protected mappen a doozen er bodies for next ta nowt. It's likely yer've heard as hoo a† defied the graave wi' Miss Undine wi' varra girt sooccess."

And then Gideon Cuyp hitched up his

* After.

† " I" is sometimes pronounced as if written " A" in both Westmoreland and Cumberland..

short leg and looked over the table as
though his self-sufficiency ought to be like
this proclaimed.

"No, indeed, Mr. Cuyp, I had not heard
of that," said the minister. "Lady D'Acth
is, of course, naturally indisposed to enter
upon a subject that is so full of pain to her.
She is a changed woman from her loss, even
though your niece is so great a comfort to
her; and I may confess to you, Mr. Cuyp,
that the interest I take in such inventions
as yours is only second to that which I
have been led to take in Miss Norman.
You will not misunderstand me. I have
known her excellent aunt for many years, and
that she should have found so sweet a charge
cannot be a matter of indifference to me."

Now Gideon Cuyp thought that he was
being practised on by the great Minister of
State, but he was not very sure.

"Weel, weel, she's a re-al bonny lass, a
bethinks ma, Mr. Massareene, for awe that a
ses it messel wo* happen suddn't. I teak'd†
her, a did, when she wur nowt bet a tinny

* Who. † Took.

thing, an' I've kip her aboot ma ivver sen, though a nivver meeak'd owt by her—nivver a harp'ny. It's trew, a promise ye."

"It does you great honour, Mr. Cuyp—great honour. Her aunt, as I have told you, is an old and a dear friend of mine; and therefore the future of this very interesting girl naturally concerns me not a little."

"She wor a deal roon'd eftre, Mr. Massareene, a site er fooak hes telt ma, oop in th' girt toon.* Bet happen ye knaa awe aboot it yerssel'."

Now Fabian Massareene in his present company did not mean to know anything—that is, anything more than was quite convenient. He had got the undertaker there to learn of him, therefore this questioning of Gideon Cuyp must not be encouraged. So he merely bowed as if in confession of his ignorance, and the undertaker went on.

"I's bin telt that she might hev hed a dooke,†—an' a deal er udthers er sooch like; an' I wes a bit vexed ta hear as hoo she wuddn't say nowt that wes pleasant to the

* Great town.   † Duke.

reechest mon in awe England. Lady
D'Aeth telt ma he cudn't hev gi'en ta her
less than hef a million er moony—it's a
serious site er brass—it is sooa : an' she telt
me he wer gittan mappen* a thoosond poonds
a day. Bet it isn't that th' lass is o'er keen,
for she isn't keen enoo—she's only gae hard
tae pleeas ;† she is, hawivver."

"But there must be some reason for this,
eh, Mr. Cuyp?" inquired the minister, who
was now assured that the undertaker knew
nothing of that which had been asked in the
long corridor. "Now, as an old friend of Lady
D'Aeth's, I have taken the liberty to suggest
to her the possibility of there being some
attachment, even in this place that she
and you are not aware of. Young ladies,
you know, Mr. Cuyp, will be their own
enemies sometimes, and even like to throw
themselves away." And after the minister
had so said he threw himself back on his
chair, and waited for the undertaker.

"Ay, ay, that's joost it, that's joost what
a bethinks ma, an' what a olas ses," eagerly

* Perhaps. † Please.

answered Cuyp, who was now fast getting off his guard; "happen soom sad, pious sort ov a mon—it's a gae mash oop aboot yon hef a meellion a moony—I isn't yusta* sick like, I's ameeast† mad."

"I quite agree with you, Mr. Cuyp; I quite begin to think there is some secret attachment. Of course it's no business of mine, but if I were *you* I'd find it out."

"Bet I's nowt ta be findin' oot, Mr. Massareene; a knaa awe aboot it. I heard yan and tudther taukin' loovin' yan‡ varra dark neet, when it wor black dark an' weendy, an' a cuddn't discern wor a wes geean, bet, in coorse, a didn't stay ta leesten."

"Then it's as I suppose, Mr. Cuyp, a younger son, with an allowance of, perhaps, a thousand a year, just to keep up appearances."

"By th' goode Lord, Mr. Massareene, it isn't evven a hoondred clear. If he's a yoonger son, a canna say; bet I's varra sure he hasn't gittan nin a kin ta him livin' —leastways a sud knaa if he hed, for a heard it frae th' mon wo burried awe his fooak."§

* Used to.   † Almost.   ‡ One.   § Folk.

"I am very sorry to hear it, Mr. Cuyp; but I was afraid it must be so—to throw herself away on such a man; it's really very sad." And the minister looked very solemn and gloomy, and thereupon did Cuyp further proceed to unbosom himself.

"Sad isn't th' word, Mr. Massareene, ta be heavin' away half a meellion er goode brass. It's a fool's trick, that's what I thinks a it—co it by its reet neeam. And wait a bit, wait till evven next Soonday's here, then she'll be geean ta his schools, an' o' maks er things, and tae playin' er his organ, an' see if she don't set her eyes on him ploomb* when he's a preachin' an' lookin' si coonin at her. An' he hasn't gittan sooa mutch as t' shillin'. I's sure he's fashed† an' flate‡ her wi' his re-leegion—I's sick er sooch stoof, I is sooa." And the undertaker in his vexation almost shrank under the table.

"But then, you see, Mr. Cuyp, he is of course aware that Miss Norman will in-herit your fortune——"

"Is he? Is he?" said Cuyp, as the

* Straight.　† Perplexed.　‡ Frightened.

greater part of him appeared with a bound from under the mahogany; "then he knaas wrong, he knaas meear than a dae messel. I hasn't putten bye nowt; I's doon o'er weel wi' th' lass ta hev meeaked any brass. It isn't likely. Th' fooles awe oop an' down weel be burried for sick a lile; they is sooa mean o'er th' funerals. They're for ivver a leavin' word that they moost be putten away cheeap, that there isn't ta be ni feathers, an' that meeaks a site er deefference. When I's telt that it moost be a quiet job, it meaans that I'm nit ta send a mon ta carry that board forrat wi' th' feathers on th' top; an' I don't bethink ma I's a hard sort er a mon. Mr. Massareene, there's sooch a deal er greetin'* o'er this pooder that it olas ends in their gettin' it for nowt, an' I canna meeak it messel for nowt, sooa I's tied tae loss aboot it. Bet asta yon, I doesn't grummal, for I's yabble† tae leeve."

"It does you great credit, Mr. Cuyp; with your feelings you can be never poor."

"Weel, weel, a won't say bet I's mebbie

* Crying.   † Able.

a bit soft a chance teem or sooa, though
a canna be as leeberal ye knaa when
there's any credit," said the cautious undertaker, who was not well persuaded but that
the minister would end by ordering some
powder.

"Of course not, Mr. Cuyp, that's not to
be expected—trade is trade, and you cannot afford to be ruined because of the
mourners. But let me say it does seem to
me to be only the more deplorable that, if
you are not in a position to make any pro-
vision for Miss Norman, she should have
thrown away so much that is substantial,
only because she has set her heart on a
hopeless and impossible attachment."

"Ay, neea doot ov 't, an' if yu'd believe
it, Mr. Massareene, he telt ta her, did this
Mr. Melchior, that he cuddn't and that he
wuddn't wed her, becos he hed nowt tae kip
her on, an' a deal meear er that sort er stoof,
bet it dudn't gammon ma ; an' then he spak'
terble loovin, an' hooged her a goode few
teems, he did, hawivver, and telt ta her he
sud olas loove her as a brudther."

" And you heard Mr. Melchior say this, Mr. Cuyp? Really, a clergyman might be otherwise occupied."

" Evven ivvery word ov't; a heard him say it awe that varra day when, as I telt ye a bit sen, it wes black deark, an' ther' wor a deal er wind stirrin'; it's as trew as I's a sittin' here."

Now Fabian Massareene had got to know nearly all he cared to ask, and, as he thought, he had let out nothing to the undertaker. And he purposed to let out nothing so long as Cuyp should sit there. He could work the wretched creature as he had been worked. It was only fit that he should be so treated. But the undertaker should not ask questions of the minister. He should be used—and then he should be flung away. Nevertheless there was the love-sick priest. He must not be let to stop looking upon Minna as he would upon a sister.

" I am interested in this lady, Mr. Cuyp, for I greatly regard Lady D'Aeth, and I much regret seeing her throw away her young affections. She will, it is to be feared, get a character for being very fanci-

ful and fickle, and it then may even end in
her remaining as she is."

. " That's evven what I ses ta messel, Mr.
Massareene, evven th' saam. I bethink ma
th' meescheef's doon ; for hasn't she bin an'
floong away, as though it wor nowt, hef a
meellion of moony? Dae'ye bethink yerssel,
Mr. Massareene, that we can be gettin' quit
er this priest. It's com omma sooden,* an' I
isn't messel."

Now this was coming to business. Fabian
Massareene did not doubt but that Guy
Melchior might be got away. But he was
also minded that the getting away of the
vicar should be Cuyp's affair, and not his.
The minister did not mean to move in
the matter, other than as he now was
moving.

" I think it is not at all impossible, Mr.
Cuyp. Let me see ; he has refused Sierra
Leone, which shows that he is perhaps lack-
ing in zeal. But for all that, he might not be
indisposed to accept some other preferment
which might be more to his mind. Now
what is your opinion, Mr. Cuyp ?"

* On me sudden.

" Why joost this, Mr. Massareene ; ye can discern it's ni goode at awe geean on in this sort er way—ni goode at awe. It'll gae soon be tae laate, if it isn't noo ; she'll be heavin' away meear goode brass eftre* yon hef a meellion. I isn't set on gettin' bock agin awe that I've putten doon o'er th' lass, teem upod teem. It isn't that, I'll warr'n ye; bet I canna bear ta see her geean a meeakin' this serious sad set. A canna, hawivver. Though I's nowt bet her ooncle, Mr. Massareene, I's th' feelin's ov a fadther in this job;" and Cuyp hid himself behind his pocket-handkerchief.

" And after all, Mr. Cuyp, the substituted parent, such a one as you have been, is often less selfishly interested than the original. I believe I am speaking to one who will not abuse my confidence, and therefore I do not hesitate to say that the husband of Miss Norman, whoever he may be, should, in my opinion, insist upon showing, in some substantial way, his appreciation of your devotedness to her. I know what you

* After.

would say, Mr. Cuyp; nevertheless I must persist in thinking that you should be handsomely remunerated. But of course this is only an opinion; it is no affair of mine, and I fear we are only talking of impossibilities so long as Mr. Melchior remains vicar of Black Moss. What do you think, Mr. Cuyp? He is, I believe, delicate, and there is nothing now, I fear, to suit him in any of our healthy colonies."

Gideon Cuyp searched through the minister, and then bodily edged himself nearer the great man. But yet that greatness did not to that furnisher of funerals seem very terrible.

"Weel, Mr. Massareene, happen a sud ta hev a lile, bet a nivvir bethowt ma aboot it afore—nivver."

"No, not a little, Mr. Cuyp, but a great deal—a good round sum—that is what I should do in such a case."

When Gideon Cuyp heard this he made a little calculation. Would it be worth his while to make this priest to go? for this he knew was what the minister had had him there to do. The minister would come down with a " round sum " if he could get the girl. Yes; it would be worth his while.

" Weel, weel, Mr. Massareene, it's goode ta see that Mr. Melchior moost begot away. I'll spak wi' him aboot it. It's a wattre* joorney that I's wantin' ta see he tak'," said Cuyp, significantly. And then he bowed to the minister and shambled out.

" He'll be doing this clergyman some violence. He's as big a rogue as there is unhung," said the minister as he went up the stairs. " At any rate he has not seen my hand."

" It wes as weel he did simma.† He's a serious soft sort ov a mon for si girt a meenister; he is, hawivver. He's awe for ma doin' tae yon priest a meescheef. He's a gae parlish rogue; he is sooa, an' he canna' discern that I knaa what he's at," said Gideon Cuyp, as he put up his gloves and dipped along beneath the beeches.

---

* Water.   † See me.

CHAPTER III.

JOB REDCAR'S SUSPICION.

ANOTHER season by now had come and nearly
gone, and yet the lowering fortunes of Black
Moss were not in the way of mending.
There were those who had believed that they
would have mended when the fever went;
but then the fever had gone, and it was
beginning to be understood that Black Moss
had been ruined. There were only a few
little shops, where such things as sweetstuff
and oat bread stood up against the casements, and this was all except the draper,
who was the biggest tradesman in the place,
and who also sold cheese, and all kinds of
groceries, and was appointed to supply the
candles for the reading-desk and the pulpit
during the winter months. And sometimes
he also displayed by the side of his brooms,

some spare-ribs after the killing of a neighbour's pig—but there was no one in Black
Moss who was a regular purveyor of any
sort of meat. Certain there were indeed
who "butched a bit noo an' then," but
they looked for their meat to a butcher who
journeyed to them from afar twice a week in
the winter, and three times in the season.
But now there was no sweetstuff for the flies
to assemble together on in the casements—
the draper called together those to whom
he owed anything, and told them that if he
had time he should certainly pay something
in the pound—and if they would not give
him time they must take his soap and candles, and even all that he had in drapery
behind the other counter. So they bethought
them that if they gave him time, the soaps
would be washed away, the candles burned,
and that the draperies would otherwise
escape them ; therefore they told him that
they could not wait, and he took off his
apron and put up his shutters.

The stricken and decimated valley had
not only lost most of its souls, but nearly all

of its character. Travellers to the country
of the lakes avoided it, or hurried scared
through the pass and the Gap, expectorating
the while if they unwittingly were taken there.
Its mountains were no longer climbed. Its
streams were unfished. The tarn trout
were in no danger whilst they fed; the dark
mosses on the hill sides were ungathered.
The little inn was unvisited, and the mountain ponies were ordered for immediate sale.
Black Moss was under a ban, and Black
Moss knew it. Again the stream flowed
purely, the stream that had flowed so terribly in that picture paper; but yet a taint
remained. No one would come so that they
might see the place was clean. And at the
last it began to be thought that the name of
Black Moss would never get to be purified.
Mr. Cropper, the neighbouring apothecary,
was entreated to write about it to the *Times*,
and he wrote accordingly; but that which
was written did not, somehow, see the light
of day. So after that, Black Moss was prepared to be wiped out.

In the midst of these dark, threatening

days, there came amongst them the great
minister from London.   It was stated every
week in the county paper that Fabian Massareene could do anything, that his power
was an amazing thing, and that the doing
of good was the business of his life.   Therefore he could lift them up again; and the
draper, who was still out of work, and wrote
a very neat, clear hand, said, one evening in
the tap-room of the Fish Inn, that he
would write to the minister if Black Moss
liked.   And Black Moss not only liked, but
gathered round him to compel him; and
presently he read out what he had written,
amidst a murmur of applause; and then he
went proudly on his way to make of it a fair
copy.   And this was the fair copy that he
made :

"Gent.*

"A knaa as a is takin' a libberty in meeakin
bold ta rite this.   Bet then a Da hear as
ya are for ivver doin' ov Good, an' that ya
wont Object.

* This is a fact.

"Gent, we are varra ni Ruind in this Spot a am sold oop, an' noo there's Joseph bivins as kips th' fish inn here he ses ta Me he cant hod on a deal langer, he ses ta ma he weel be forcd ta Drop it we hev hed th' fever orful bad, an' noo it's geean Away, an' there isn't nae smels. Bet nae yan wont coom ni oos they wont, hawivver.

"Gent, as a am th' best scholard in this spot a deal of fooak as knaas ma hes exd ma ta rite this, soaa ive rit it, cos it aint rite noo hoo, that we sud be gettin' Mashed oop noo th' fever is geean, ta ex ya gent ta spak For oos when ya are gettin' back ta Lunnun an' say as hoo we are cleean agin an' that we cant gie th' Fever ta nin. A sends yan a me cards that ya may Discern* a is respectable an' if ya weel spak' this a sall Open agin Mr. Cropper that's oor pothcay ses we aint noon ov oos fectious, an' that we are Sweet Bet nae coompany weel coom ni oos if ye wont spak' for

---

* This is a favourite expression amongst the lower classes in Cumberland.

oos I is gent yar oomble Servant john tibbs."

And the answer of the minister filled with hope the breast of John Tibbs, and when it was read in the tap-room, Joseph Bivins of the Fish Inn, resolved that he would yet hold on, and not order out the ponies for immediate sale.

Gideon Cuyp was the while beginning, little by little, to be the less disquieted about the remote possibility of his having to account for what he had done ; the vicar had come to tell him about Sierra Leone, which was a friendly thing to do ; and he could also see that, other than this, Guy Melchior did not seem to desire to accuse him. He did not believe that this priest had followed up the suspicion which had once so compassed him about ; and the undertaker, on the whole, was satisfied that the present calm would not be disturbed to his undoing ; therefore he once again put himself in the way of meeting the vicar ; and it was otherwise easy to see that most of his fear had gone

out of him. And had he not concluded
rightly that his character in that place was
not to be touched by any shock? Had not
his life through been a lie—that is, one un-
detected lie? Had he not these many years
been building up an excellent and a convenient name upon his alms and his charities, that would not easily be overset by the
witness of this coat? Would not any such
suspicion the rather recoil upon those who
might unadvisedly project it? And Job
Redcar, a sinner and the friend of sinners,
would that which he might say, if he ever
again came out of his bed, be regarded other
than as a crime—a fitting top to all his
vices? So it may be seen that Gideon
Cuyp in those days had greatly taken heart,
and went about with more of the manner
that he once did wear. And then he was
very often at the Abbey, and made his dinner
when his friends there lunched, which was
a saving to himself, which fell, however,
hardly on the hag who made his bed. And
once she did tell Cuyp that she was hun-
gered; "I hasn't hed a bit er meeat sen

Moondy ; I's fuirly hoongered, I is that,"
and the poor lean, worn-out woman looked
voracious.

" I bethinks ma ya is fat enoo ; ya hes a
terble stoomach for meeat, an' ya's for ivver
hoongered when I's foole. Ya hes a deal
er vittuls."

" Then I canna stay, for I's fairly nowt
imma."*

" Then ya can gea th' waays ; ya'r goode
for nowt."

And such as this had often passed between them since they first had come together; but she never left him.   His
hard reproach was true ; she *was* good for
nothing, for had she not broken down in the
doing of his work ?

Gideon Cuyp was ever insolent when he
concluded he was safe ; and now he concluded none could harm him. And then did
he not call up his subscriptions and his
benefactions—did he not sniff the fragrance
of his many virtues, and were he accused,
would they not be sniffed by others ?   There-

* In me.

fore he took his ease, and set his heel upon his hireling.

Now it was very true that Guy Melchior, thinking less and less, as time went on, of the unlikely guilt of Gideon Cuyp, had not prosecuted his suspicion to any issue. He had struggled to be rid of it, and he had not been wholly unsucessful. The vicar knew that he had stumbled about Minna, and it was on his mind that in that matter he had fallen terribly away, and was only a very weak shepherd for his sheep—therefore he would now be careful to bridle up his tongue. So he reasoned within himself that the giving of that coat to Job Redcar bore upon it rather the seeming of accident than of intention. It could not be suffered him to think that the man whose going in the face of all men had been so straight, purposed to have murder on his hands. Nor could he the better set down to trace the changing of the bottle by his bed-side to the work of the undertaker. And yet there was much that was not clear, and that he dared not think of. Then, too, he inquired of himself, Was it fit that he should so accuse this man of that which was so grave, when there rested so much doubt upon his purpose? Did it beseem him as a clergyman to do this thing? And when he had inquired of himself, the answer that he got was " No."

But whilst the vicar, after this sort, was concerned to get rid of the suspicion, Job Redcar, the while, was possessed by it, and was minded that he would accuse the under-taker. Guy Melchior had remembered the many noble acts that Cuyp had done—how he had fed the hungry, and clothed the naked, and he said, "The man who could live as this one has lived, can set his life against this accusation. There is a bare suspicion, but there is nothing more; and shall not his virtues stand before the thought that would suspect him of so foul a thing?" And so the vicar let it stand. But then Job Redcar was only a "swiller,"* and that did not hold him which did refrain the priest. Laid upon his bed for months by a wasting and terrible sickness, the fate that had nearly come on him through the contriv-ing of the undertaker was, in the mind of Job,

* Basket-maker.

an unresting and an assured conviction. He
never had believed in Gideon Cuyp, as had
so many in Black Moss. The coffin-maker
had never been other than as a "whited
sepulchre" to Job. He had watched Cuyp
climb, and he knew that every step the climber
took was planted upon some fresh fraud;
therefore he was very sure that in the
coming of that coat there was a meaning.
He had never told to others that which he
had seen in Cuyp, for in men's hearts and
minds the undertaker stood too strongly to
be overset. Job, as yet, had held his peace,
but now he thought upon his bed that he
would have his say.

His little cottage, set high upon a dreary
fell, was some distance from Black Moss;
and even had he intended before to have
told to others that which he suspected, he
had had, throughout his long and torturing
confinement, scarcely the opportunity. The
people in those parts, in these times, had
hurried quickly past each other, and such
very inconsiderable intercourse as Job Redcar
might at any time have had with his distant
neighbours in the valley was, during his

sickness, entirely cut off. And then the
vicar, when he came, did not lead Job to in-
troduce these bitternesses of which the swiller was reported to be full. Guy Melchior
came to that cottage on the great business
of good will amongst men; and when Job
sat up, and, with the little strength he had,
was set on saying hard and bitter things,
the vicar would seek to make smooth Job's
thoughts, the while he smoothed his pillow.
Therefore Job had been a good deal let and
hindered when he would have spoken to
the vicar against Gideon Cuyp.

Long after Job's sore sickness had been
pronounced by Mr. Cropper to be mortal
and his recovery hopeless, to the amazement
of the few herdsmen and miners that ever
came near him, Job began to amend. Mr.
Cropper, when he saw the man who should
have died so very likely to live, ran out and
said it was a miracle, and not the working
of his drugs.

"Nae, nae, I's thinkin' varra sendry,*
Meester Cropper. Whaar sud a hev gantull†

---

* Different.   † Gone to.

bet for th' beer? It's evven th' beer that I suddn't ha' sooped."

Now one of Mr. Cropper's first proceedings had been to stop Job Redcar's beer, for Job was of a full habit; but nevertheless Job had never ceased to drink it from that time until the day when Mr. Cropper had run out to testify about the miracle.

" You mean to tell me, Job, you've never stopped your beer ?"

" That's evven what a meean, Meester Cropper."

"Amazing ! And in so bloated a patient!" And the little man could not hide his agitation, for he knew that in this matter he had been beaten by the beer.

" Ya is happen a lile warrm, Meester Cropper. Sall a teem* ya oot a soop er portre ?"† And Job rose in his bed to offer his hospitality, and produced a bottle from beneath his pillow.

" And this is what you've been drinking, Job?" asked the apothecary, tasting the liquor.

" A ne nowt else, sartanly, Meester Cropper. Joost a glass when a wes dry."

* Pour.   † Porter.

" But then, you're always dry."

" A chance teem a is, Meester Cropper; bet I isn't sick a baad yan as them totallers ses."

" I suppose you took a glass to your dinner, Job ?"

" And mebbie two happen meear, an' aboot th' like at soopper ; an' joost an odd yan when I's dry ; bet nivver meear than ten of any day, Meester Cropper—that's trew, I'll warrn ya."

" Ten glasses !" ejaculated the appalled apothecary, as he seized his hat and fled. " Wouldn't this startle them at Guy's !" Now, Mr. Cropper's skill was got into him at Guy's.

When Fabian Massareene was staying at the Abbey, Job Redcar was well able to go about again ; and then it was that the fixed purpose, which had never for a moment•left him, was to be worked out. He had heard, as he first went out upon the fells, how that the interference of the minister had been asked in solemn form by John Tibbs, with a view to the getting back of some of the public confidence and disbursements to Black

Moss ; and it seemed to him that this was a likely and a promising time to float his untiring suspicion.

It was one evening early in August that he so resolved to make a trial of his intention, and as it was getting to be dusk he set out for Black Moss. The summer air was soft and cool as he came down the fell side, and he thought that he had strength sufficient for that which he had to do. And he felt as he got into the Gap, that even the weakness which had for so many months been on him could not send him back. To many, who had long heard that he must die, and had given him over to the grave, his appearance on that summer night, when the shadows were creeping out, was as that of an apparition.

" Why, if it isn't th' spurrit ov puir Job," said one, who in the twilight had seen the swiller pass. But Job heard it, and stopped to show that he was abroad in the flesh.

"If it's his spurrit he cud soop a lile portre—he cud sooa," said Job, showing that one of the lusts of the flesh was yet strong

on him. "Hoo is't wi' ye, Tom, an' th'
missis?"

"Joost meedlin', Job: teems is gae baad,
bet I's glaad ta see ya isn't ta dee. Mr.
Cropper a while sin' ses he cudn't kip yer
wick."*

"An' that's trew; he had lile enoo wi' th'
kippin o' ma wick, a promees ya. It waar
th' beer, Tom, that's doon it." And after this
Job never stopped till he got into Black Moss.

It soon came to be told that Job Redcar
had "takken oop," and was drinking
mulled ale at the Fish Inn. One after
another did such of his old friends as had
escaped the fever turn in to see him, that
they might judge whether it was indeed the
swiller in the flesh, or a counterpart who
had come to steal away their congratulations
and their beer money; and it was well that
Mr. Cropper did not chance to see how
many times Job's mug was filled, as he was
pronounced to be the real man.

"Sooa there's ni fooak stirrin' aboot,
Joseph?" inquired Job of the landlord.

* Alive.

"Nae, Job, nae, an' that be th' trewth ; hey! they'rs bin sick teems as a nivvir knaad —nivvir. It's bin plaguey baad wi' awe er oos, a reckon; awe bet Gideon Cuyp——"

Job Redcar would then have had his say concerning that which the landlord had spoken ; but the host of the Fish was carrying his ale to other customers.

As it presently got darker, most of the principal villagers had assembled in the tap-room. Their talking, which was quite sufficiently wetted, turned chiefly upon the present calamitous position and prospects of Black Moss ; and Job, who was accounted to be shrewd by all who knew him, was invited to pronounce an opinion on John Tibbs' "letter to the minister."

"Wyah, ov coorse I's messel ; I isn't John Tibbs, is a, John? Bet I'd be lettin' th' girt meenister aleean, an' I'd joost start questin wo as bin at th' bottom er this fever."

"Wyah, th' Lord's sent oos th' plague, Job; th' goode Lord ta bat* oos wi' his

---

* Beat or chide.

loove, an' nin beside, I'll warr'n oos," said an old man, reverently.

"Nae, nae, Abraham, ye's meestakken terble; a knaa varra sendry ta yon." And then Job got up and came close to the old man, and said, "Looke ye, Abraham; it wasn't th' goode Lord as bristed* th' draan oop yonder, aside er beck, an' sent oos th' fever ta soop; an' it wesn't, a tak' it, th' goode Lord neither that sent ma a co-at that wes evven wick wi' fever." And Job shook his head mysteriously, and then got back to his beer.

Now they all knew, from the beginning, that Job had something on his mind, and there was a little whispering amongst them; and then John Tibbs went up to the swiller.

"Yar telts oos, Job, that it canna be th' Lord's doin' as bristed th' draan, an' it's goode enoo ta see that ya knaa wo'st doon oos this serious mees-cheef. Coom, coom, Job, an' let's be hearin' awe aboot it."

---

* Burst.

† The word "who," amongst the lower classes in Cumberland and Westmoreland, is pronounced wo.

"Ay, ay, Job; be doin' as John exes ya," said the old man who was called Abraham, seeing that Job answered nothing.

"Weel, weel, Abraham, ya sall awe be telt what a knaas aboot it. It's a serious mees-cheef, trew enoo, as John ses, an' a sad yan, there's nae dispute on't; an' he's a gae releegious sort a marpie as has doon it. Yar'll be bethinkin' yerssels I's crackin' on ya likely when I's telt oot his neeam," said Redcar, coming into the midst of his eager listeners, and searching their faces.

"Nae, nae, Job, it isn't ya wo'd be crackin' er oos," put in John Tibbs, trustfully. "Ya isn't a ploomp leear,* Job."

"As ya weel hev it, ya moost, me lads," said Job, turning a little pale. "Weel, then, leeak,† it's for ivver Gideon Cuyp;" and they all fell back, and looked unbelievingly on the speaker of such words.

Then there was silence for awhile, and Joseph Bivins almost let fall some liquor he

* Great liar. . † Look.

was bringing in when he heard the fearful thing with which Job Redcar charged the undertaker. Then he put down his glasses, and went sternly up to Job, for he bethought him he might have to answer for this which was spoken at the Fish.

"I's glaad ta see ya agin, Job, I is that; an' ya's fetched ma loock,* for I's fool er company ta neet, bet a canna bear this wrong telt er Gideon Cuyp."

"That's reet, Joseph. Job's mappen a lile weakly, or he wuddn't likely be sooa varra silly," put in the old man Abraham.

"I durst bet ya a harp'ny, Job, it canna be he—it canna be he. Ya wudn't crack on oos, we knaa that varra weel; but it's faancy, it is, hawivver, an' nowt else. Let's drap this tauk, me lads—let's drap it. He's a re-al goode sort er mon, is Gideon Cuyp. He'd ha' meeaked a gae preacher."

"Ay, that's for ivver trew; he's far o'er goode for sick a job, is Gideon Cuyp," said one.

"Sooa foole a comfortable Bible tauk," put in a second.

* Luck.

"An' sooa free wi' his brass," added a third.

"Sooa keen aboot th' puir fooak awe oop an' down, an' th' hoongered," testified a fourth.

And this and much more like to it rose up to meet the first appearance in public of Job Redcar's suspicion.

Job, however, who had for some time pondered over the possibility of his suspicion being met with this sort of demonstration, was not to be put back either by the authority of Joseph Bivins, or by any lesser terror. He was not going to drop it; and he would do that which he was set on doing even if it was not fit to be spoken at the Fish. He knew how many voices would be lifted up to speak for Cuyp. For that he was prepared; but he had not prepared himself for the authority of Bivins, and he did not mean that the publican should stop him.

"Joost as't pleases ya, Joseph; if a mudn't spak' here, a mappen* may at th' Cross Keys;"

* I perhaps.

and Job as he said this moved towards the door.

Now the Cross Keys was not a pleasant place to Joseph Bivins, for it kept away many of the Red Moss swillers from the Fish; therefore it was a necessity that Job Redcar should be soothed.

"Weel, it's mebbie reet that Job sud a be spakin' sick as he knaas; he canna dae a meescheef ta Meester Cuyp, that's sure."

"Ay, ay, Joseph," said many voices. And then it was permitted Job to speak.

"If a deedn't noo bethink ma yu'd be awc cleean fashed when a telt yer. Bet it fairly caps ma if a don't ameeast bottom it afoore I's doon; it weel that. Whist noo, whist noo, me lads, an' I'll telt ya a lile aboot it. He sends oop ta ma, does Cuyp, wi' th' parson, a girt brown co-at that wor foul an' rank we th' fever. He did it er poorpose."

"Ya canna prove it, Job, ya canna that," said John Tibbs.

"But ya's in sick a hoorry, mon, for I's

geean ta prove it;" and then he went out,
and came back with the coat.

Instantly, the some-time owner of the
coat was proclaimed aloud by many tongues.

"Weel, weel, ma lads, dudn't a say sooa
a bit sen, when Joseph yonder wor for
meeakin' ma drap it? an' dudn't ya bethink
yerssels a wor telling a ploomp lee? An'
I'll joost ex ya noo, wesn't this th' co-at er
feeve* dead yans afoore it ivver coom'd rank
er it's fire tama?" And Job Redcar held
up the co-at triumphantly, for he felt that
he should conquer; and he also knew that
he had something yet to tell.

"It was evven Toomas's co-at a while sen,
Toomas as died er th' fever. I'll ensure it,"
said one.

"An' it waar Danel's an' Robert's eftre
Toomas waar burried," witnessed another.

"Bet that's nowt; that doesn't coople
Cuyp wi' th' co-at. I's sure he dudn't knaa
th' co-at waar rank er fever," still asserted
the old man Abraham.

"There ya's for ivver wrong, Abraham,"

* Five.

H 2

said Job; "dudn't Gideon Cuyp bury awe
feeve er 'em? dudn't he strip 'em? dudn't
he strip th' co-at o'er feeve er th' bodies?
When yan wur dead, dudn't he say he'd burrn
their clothes? an' dudn't he send this co-at
ta a gae lock er fooak awe oop an' doon?
An' what's meear an' a deal worse, dudn't he
gie th' co-at ta th' pure vicar ta tak' timma?*
Ye canna say he dudn't, ye canna that?"

It was felt by all assembled at the Fish
that in this matter it would be hard to answer to Job Redcar's suspicion. Gideon
Cuyp, it was very true, had performed these
last offices, and had taken upon himself to
get rid of the infected clothes. And it was
now beginning to be seen with what intention he had been so busy. The reaction, slow
to start, was now fast setting in. Job Redcar's suspicion was doing its work, and that in
time seemed likely to become infectious.

"It looks orful baad agin he, bet he's saaf
ta clear hissel," said Joseph Bivins.

"He's sick a re-al releegious sort er a mon,
also a prayin', an' gieen away broken vit-

* To me.

tuls. Nae, nae, it canna be Gideon Cuyp,"
said John Tibbs, rather weakly.

"Bet then, a hasn't telt ya awe ; there's
meear that's block enoo ta coom," put in
Job Redcar, who saw that, for all they tried
to shake off the suspicion, it was still clinging about some. "That isn't awe. I's cracken
nowt a promus ya. Gideon Cuyp's nowt ta
ma, only he isn't geean ta cleean cap ma
wi' his serious hypocritin'. Dudn't th' girt
doctor wo waar fetched to see Mees Undine,
dudn't he say summut about its bein' varra
straange that th' wattre waar sooa gae queer?
an' dudn't he ex wo wor inspectur? an'
when Cuyp ses ta he, It's them rats, dudn't
Cuyp drap doon his neb* as though he waar
flate,† for ivver joost th' saam as a dissenter
dae when he roons agin a choorchman ?"

"Ay, ay, sure he did, noo a bethinks
ma," said Sawrey Knotts, the sexton.

Many of those who stood round Redcar
were now less willing to weigh what might
fall from the swiller, or it would have been
clear to them that there was very little

* Head.　　　† Frightened.

against Cuyp in this story of the rats. But the belief in the undertaker's guilt, which at the first they would none of them persuade themselves to look at, was now getting to be very strong, with every symptom of becoming presently very active and personal. Job had filled them with his own suspicion, and that which a while before they would not listen to, they now accepted eagerly; and those who still hesitated to condemn the undertaker dared hardly think about that coat. Nevertheless, upon the whole, things were not getting to look well for Gideon Cuyp.

" Bet then, Job," said John Tibbs, " there isn't tied ta be mitch in yander aboot th' raats. The doctor dudn't bethink him that Gideon Cuyp did sick a saad treek* as put 'em in yon spot; an' what's meear, them raats hed nowt ta dae wi' th' fever."

" Bet a say they hed, John; they burrur'd away an' away evven betwixt them two draans; that's hoo them raats wark'd for Gideon Cuyp."

" An' if they mappen did meeak them

* Trick.

holes yander, th' raats waar nowt ta Gideon
Cuyp. He nivver hed nooa raats."

· "Ay, bet then a knaad he hed, an' joost
at yon teem, noo a bethinks ma," put in
Sawrey Knotts; "for a seed 'em messel, an'
hoongered enoo they waar on· a lile tinny
soop er podish."*

"Weel, weel, Sawrey, that's like enoo, a
isn't disputin' it; but then that don't say as
hoo he started them raats ta meeak th' hole,"
still pleaded John Tibbs, who was yet loyal
to the undertaker.

"There ya's reet, John; a dudn't see he
put th' varmin in th' wattre."

"I knaad ya dudn't, Sawrey," broke in
John Tibbs, exultingly.

"Stay a bit, John; I's only slow. Ya
is o'er fest† foma;‡ that's evven trew as a
dudn't see it doon; bet a dud see him once
o'er when it waar a gae black neet, coomin'
aleeang frae behint th' graaves wi' a caage
rank wi' raats in his hend; a cud varra ni
hev tooched them messel, an' a see him gea
doon ta th' draan, an' a wes capped wi' th'

* Porridge.   † Fast.   ‡ For me.

job, bet dudn't bethink messel what he waar doin'."

"I canna believe wrong er him," still persisted plain John Tibbs; "he olas stook tama, wud hev noon oother cannels* for th' choorch bet mine. It isn't likely he'd dae sick a treek."†

"He'd do joost owt he waar minded ta fill his coffins, an' that's for ivver wyah he dud this job. It is sooa," rejoined Redcar. "It wud breeng he a gae lock er brass, a guess."

They had all given the undertaker over now; even John Tibbs would make no sign. The past was coming back to them, and they saw things then as they never had before; they only remembered how the place had been desolated. They had heard these stories of the coat and the rats; they did not ask of themselves how much was doubtful and how little was proved; but they had been put upon the scent, and they proposed to deal terribly with Gideon Cuyp when they should get him. They rushed at Job Redcar's suspicion,

---

* Candles.   † Trick.

and almost with one voice adopted it. They would be Cuyp's accusers, his judges and his executioners. No man should take him out of their hands. And some cried for one vengeance and some for another, but many cried that they would kill him. Many remembered how the scourge had blighted them. How that before it came their homes rang with little voices, and were warm with a wife's smile; and they remembered too, each one for himself, that in his home now there was a terrible and a withering void. And *he* had done this thing; *he* had taken away their peace, and swept away their life's joys. And they rose up with a yell and said that they would have him.

"He's evven left ma nin ; th' aald ooman* an' me bairns are awe geeand."

"They waar three re-al bonny lasses waar meen, an' there isn't a wick yan left."

"It's varra bad, John, bet I's a deal worse. You've meear coomfort left, a conny bit, for hasn't a loss ma wife as weel ?"

"An' it's ma lile tinny yans that he's bin

* Woman.

an' claimed er ma.　I's fairly aleean, there isn't a sound at heeam."*

So did each one tell to his fellow how he had been bereaved.　And then there was a whispering as though the worst had not even yet been spoken.

"If this be trew as Job as telt oos, an' a knaa a deal is, Cuyp's bin an' takken th' life er oor blessed yoong lady, he's kilt Meess Undine."

And as the sexton declared this deduction of his to the taproom, a shout of execration came up from every throat; a shout, too, that would have spoken fearfully to Gideon Cuyp, if he could have heard its savage ring.

"An' noo, ma lads," said Job, starting to his feet, "what sall we dae wi' he?"

It was an awful question as it then was uttered, and only one voice asked to give him justice.

"Let's hear he hissel," said John Tibbs. And other than John Tibbs no one interposed a thought or a gesture of mercy. They were athirst and cried for blood, and a stronger man than John Tibbs could not now have held them back.

* Home.

"Put he at tarn—droon he wi' a girt coble!* Put he at tarn whaar it's black deep! Ta th' tarn wi' Gideon Cuyp!" And they crowded round the swiller as he shouted out the undertaker's awful doom. There was no one then who could have turned them from their terrible resolve.

"Sure bet yer a soft un an' a sorry, John, to be speakin' sick stooff," said Job to Tibbs, as he almost overset the grocer-draper. And after this sort, headed by Job Redcar, they all roughly took their way to the house of Gideon Cuyp. One voice still urged "Tak' he ta th' joodge," but it was lost in the cry of "Tak' he ta th' tarn!" Then John Tibbs, seeing that these men would proceed of their own accord to be Cuyp's executioners, being peacefully disposed, bethought him that he had said enough for the coffinmaker, and so went back into the Fish, and held his peace.

The long and heavy floods had swollen the waters of the tarn, and they were already far

* Stone.

up in the valley, and the little moon there was showed that they were rising fast.

"He'll hev tae be swimmin' terble lofty wi' back oot he neet,* a reckon; he weel, hawivver," said Job, as he led on to the undertaker's cottage. And with these and other like refreshers of their hate, they reached Cuyp's door.

"Whist!" said the swiller, as they gathered round the house; "whist, ma lads, or we sall flate† he. It's a gae clim, bet it isn't for nowt."

The summons to open to them was answered slowly by the old woman who served the coffinmaker's meals and made his bed.

"There's a goode few er ya, a tak' it, ta be questin th' maister this teem a neet ; bet he's geeand oot a bit sen, an' noo he hesn't coomd back."

"It isn't trew ye be telling oos, mudther; he's bethowt him why wa's coomd, an' he's mappen gittan th' start a oos; or he's lygin'‡ in yan a his ain coffins," said Job,

* Night.   † Frighten.   ‡ Lying.

fiercely ; for the swiller began to think that his suspicions after all would not end in blood.

" Let's quest he, ma lads ;" and at these words, beaten and baulked, they streamed in. Not a corner was there that they did not search—even the coffins were overset to see if Cuyp was hidden in one of his own shells.

" Whist ! whist ! ma lads," said Sawrey Knotts ; " he be likely enoo skoolkin' in th' graave-yard—he's a deal er teems there er neets ;" and on this fresh scent they went towards the burying-ground.

" We'll hev he yet, I'll warr'n oos ; he sall na crappen* oot this once ; he shan't, hawivver," said Job Redcar, as they poured along.

" I'se telt 'em wrong ; he be geeand ta Meester Melchior ; they'd doon he a mess-cheef likely, for they're most beered oop. Sawrey was evven rank er drink, bet they's saaf ta meest† he noo," chuckled the old woman, after that they had disappeared and were lost in the night.

* Creep.   † Safe to miss.

CHAPTER IV.

BY THE TARN.

When Gideon Cuyp had that evening at the
Abbey counselled Fabian Massareene to send
Guy Melchior on a longish water journey,
he had this purpose before him. He was
minded that if the vicar would not go of his
own accord beyond the seas, then that his
journeying should begin, and should end, in
the tarn. He had not suddenly come to this
resolve. Cruel, and mean, and false he had
ever been. From many he had taken away
the little that was theirs to take; but, until
now, he had never thought to take away
another's life. When it had come into his
mind to do this thing, he, at the first, held
back. It had crept on him, and the feeling
was new, and it must be said it was not nice
to him. Nevertheless, after he had struggled

for a little against it, it began to have a nicer seeming; and then, too, he got that terrible letter which told him how that the half a million of money and the thousand pounds a day had been declined, as though it were nothing that they should have been offered. Therefore when next the thought came creeping on him, he concluded that business might come of it, and he did not drive it away.

Yet, for all that he had so persuaded himself, to quiet certain scruples, Gideon Cuyp resolved to give to the vicar yet another chance. " I's a deal o'er saft for sick a job; I hasn't a site er ploock," said the undertaker, when he bethought him he would save Guy Melchior if he could. " I's fairly wick* wimmat† feelin's. I's a gae bit o'er tender—I is sooa." But if the vicar, after he had had another chance, was still immoveably minded to stay on at Black Moss, then did Gideon Cuyp determine that this much feeling should not master him. Then he resolved he would be rid of this priest at

* Alive. † With my.

once and for ever. On the whole he conceived that he was doing very nobly in this
matter.

Now it so chanced that the line that was
reported to have clean gone out, and to be
buried away under Gideon Cuyp's accumu-
lations, was found not to be so extinguished.

A survivor who had reached to great
length of days, had appeared, successfully
asserting certain remote relations. After
which the old man had laid him down and
died ; and at his death, which came to him
suddenly and easily, and when he was resting
in his chair, they brought him to lie on the
top of his fore-elders in Black Moss churchyard. It a good deal disturbed the peace
of Gideon Cuyp to hear of this coming.
His box would have to be carried away, to
give place to this old gentleman, or the old
gentleman would be let down on to his box.
In this perplexity he found some comfort
and assurance when he remembered the
sexton's great simplicity. Had it not been
for his exceeding trust in the unquestioning
and child-like docility of Sawrey Knotts in

doing such things as it was bidden him to do, Gideon Cuyp would somehow have contrived to dig the grave himself. He felt it, however, to be, on the whole, a measure of sufficient caution to look on the work of the shovel and the pick, and to see, with excellently well assumed indifference, that the sexton did not make the pit even by a foot too deep.

"Ya's a bit takken oop wi' this graave, Meester Cuyp," said Sawrey from out of the hole.

"I's capped wi' this aald mon coomin' when it waar telt oos there waar ni meea ta be fetched here."

"I bethowt ma ya waar mappen looken for summut, Meester Cuyp."

"Nae, nae, Sawrey, I's thinkin' varra sendry; there's nowt ta discern bet bones in sick a spot as this."

"A chance teem in these spots, I's bin telt, there's a deal er brass fint : a nivver fint nin messel : a dudn't, hawivver."

"There's a site er 'em stories, Sawrey," said Cuyp from the top, thinking it better to laugh, and also thinking it to be quite as well to stay. So he stopped on till Sawrey Knotts reported that he was within a foot of a coffin lid.

"That'll be ni' enoo, Sawrey, or ye'll mebbie brist* it;" for Cuyp knew the coffin to be none other than his own buried treasure. And then Sawrey Knotts made the old gentleman's bed to look very neat, and afterwards proceeded to come up out of it.

The funeral had been set down for noon the next day, as the remains were to be brought from some distance, and Gideon Cuyp had therefore resolved to carry away his gathering the night before. On his road to the grave he meant to stop at the vicarage, and then if Guy Melchior could be got, of his own choosing, to go across the seas, there would be no occasion for that journey in the tarn. But the vicar would have to make up his mind what he would do that evening. If he waited till the morrow he would wait too long. Now Cuyp did not much care which way it was. He was not

* Burst.

sure but that, perhaps, the vicar would be safer in the tarn.

It was nearly the time of the beginning of Job Redcar's *lévée* at the Fish when the undertaker reached the vicarage. Guy Melchior had just come in, and Cuyp was not kept waiting. The vicar was in his study, and there the undertaker was invited to go.

" I bethowt ma I'd joost drap in, Meester Melchior, ta tell ya that Meester Massarecne waar sayin' ta ma last neet, as hoo he waar takken wi' ya a deal, an' that he'd like terble weel ta skift ya away frae this spot an' gie ya summut graand ; he's coomin' aboot it hissel, he telt ma. He fairly cracks* on ya, he canna gie o'er crackin'—he canna that." And then Cuyp hitched himself up on to a tall chair, for he was full of his work, and did not well know what he was at.

The vicar had not lately been well pleased when he remembered how he had suspected Cuyp, and now he was very sure he had not acted in that matter as any Christian should,

---

* A common expression to signify that one is very much pleased with another.

much more a Christian with the cure of souls. Therefore his answer to the under-taker was very warm indeed.

"Mr. Massareene does me great honour to think so well of my poor services, and is very kind; and I feel that it is very good of you, Mr. Cuyp, to be the bearer of his friendly words; but are you not all my dear friends in this place? Upon yourself, Mr. Cuyp, I am sure I can rely."

And the reliable friend, at this little speech, which for him, on that occasion, was getting to be warm, wagged his shortest leg, and then, wholly overcome, came off the tall chair, and dipped up and down about the vicar.

"I's only a puir, plaan sort ov mon, Meester Melchior; bet a bethinks ma I's trew, an' a sticker; I dae hawivver."

"I *know* that, Mr. Cuyp, and I value the kindness of your call to-night; but I am so well contented here, that really I have no wish for change."

"That's trew enoo, Meester Melchior; th' pleeace is a bit dool,* an' there's a deal

* Dull.

er rain teem upod teem ; bet it's a gae nice
sort ov a spot, an' we don't nin er oos
want ta loss ya. There's only this tudther
side that mappen cud be ment* ; a hoonderd
poonds a year is a serious lile, a terble lile ;
we wants ya ta be stoppen, a promus ya,
bet it isn't reet ya sud be beggaring yerssel
for oos; we canna ex it—a bethink ma ya sud
evven be takkin' what th' girt mœenister
may be giein ya."

" Mr. Cuyp, I have made trusty and
warm friends here—my heart is in my work ;
if I went away, I should leave my heart
and my sympathies in Black Moss. And
I would not, believe me, exchange for any
consideration that would merely add to my
means, and that would also take me from
England, for I understood from Mr. Massareene that that which he had to offer me
was not in this country. My health too,
Mr. Cuyp, at present indisposes me to make
a move. I am not strong enough to under-
take new work, therefore I feel that it
would be useless now to press these kind-
nesses upon me any further."

* Mended.

Now, every word of this had urged
Cuyp on to send the vicar on that water
journey. Had not the priest out of his own
mouth confessed he had made warm friends
here; that his heart was in his work;
and that his heart would cleave to Black
Moss, wherever he might go? Yet, if it
so cleaved, it mattered nothing if he went
across the seas. No, he would do that other
thing; the Vicar of Black Moss should not
be preferred.

Now Gideon Cuyp had got to know all
that he had gone there that night to learn,
therefore he set himself to see how his work
might so be done that it could not fail.
He would set himself to see that when the
cry went up there should be none to help;
that when the flood did come there should
be no escape. Cuyp was getting to be warm
about this deed he meant to do.

" It's varra sad, Meester Melchior, varra
sad that yer heealth isn't in th' way er takkin' oop.* It's a terble cough that's bin
gettin' hod er ya. Noo, a joost bethink ma
it canna be sooa weel for ye t' be geean oop

* Hold.

an' doon them steps ; it's tied ta be doin'
ya a meeschief; joost try sleepin' doon a
bit; it's sad wark er neets to be going sooa
mooch aboot."

And Cuyp said this much as a father
would entreat a son whom he loved with
an exceeding love; there was that in the
tone of his voice which sounded genial, and
faithful, and true. And the vicar was
touched, and he showed that those words
had found him out. It was at such times
that Guy Melchior never ceased to grieve
because of the suspicion that had been once
so strong on him. Why did this man think
these little things about his cough if he did
not wish him well? He felt that he had
done to Cuyp a wrong—that he wronged
him terribly to Minna Norman. When
next he met with Minna he would tell to
her how greatly he had slipped and sinned.
So he came up to the undertaker and took
him warmly by the hand. "Mr. Cuyp,"
he said, "I once thought you did not wish
me well; can you forgive me, for now I do
believe I have not got a truer friend?"

"Forgie ya, Meester Melchior? nae,

nae, I's bet a sorry yan ta be forgieen th'
like er ya. I's glaad ya's gettin' ta be
thinkin' weel er ma, a is that; a is, hawivver."

And he looked full, and steadily, and
benevolently into the vicar's face; and he
grasped the hand that was held out there,
and grasped it with what seemed a loyal
grasp. He knew he should not be found to
flinch when the time was fully come; and
it was coming on apace, and now he was
not flinching.

"It's very good of you, my friend, to be
thinking about me, but I have not slept upstairs for some time now—I always sleep in
the next room."

Now Gideon Cuyp, from this confession,
had plumbed the depth. He had learnt how
high the waters of the tarn must rise.
Guy Melchior should start on his long journeying that night, after that he was asleep.
Cuyp knew this man would never see the
morrow; but yet he lingered on, and spoke
of things beyond the rising of the sun.
The one thing that he once had feared was

no longer a terror to him now. If the vicar, the rising of these waters notwithstanding, should, by any chance, be saved, Cuyp would not be suspected. But this did not hinder Cuyp from looking to those things by which it would be impossible to fail. And then, as it was getting to be late, he bethought him he would get up and go.

"Good night, Mr. Cuyp, and I thank you for this visit," said the vicar, very cordially and heartily indeed, the while pressing the hand that even then, that even at that parting, was held out to him. And as he spoke he lighted the undertaker to the door. "It is these floods, I fancy, that are keeping me back—you see the tarn is almost at my door." And the glare of the vicar's little lamp showed to them the heavy mists that were rolling and sweeping over the full tarn.

"Ay, ay, Meester Melchior, an' there'll be meear rain by mornin', I's thinkin'; summut sud be tried, an' soon an' awe, for th' tarn's a deal o'er ni' to be weel; it is sooa. It weel evven be droonin' ya soom day; it

weel, I'll warr'n oos, or ye'll mebbie be forced
ta sweem."*

"But then you know I'm a good swimmer,
Mr. Cuyp; good night," and the vicar closed
the door; and as it so closed upon the
playfully-delivered warning—the last Cuyp
ever meant to speak to Guy—he limped on
into the heavy damps in the direction of the
churchyard, sometimes stopping to rub his
hands and hold communion with himself,
sometimes to look back upon the waters of
the tarn on which the moon was shining
through the mists, chuckling the while some
raptures; and as his crooked and withered
body shambled along, it scarcely seemed
more hideous than grotesque. The rain had
not many hours ceased. The late heavy
floods had gained upon the tarn, and it was
yet being fed from every side by the charged
mountain streams and runners. When
Gideon Cuyp had left the vicarage, the
waters there were so far out that they almost
washed against the wicket at the back;
the evening, although there was a moon,

* Swim.

seemed early to be dark for the time of year, and Cuyp reckoned that he might with safety to himself, and without prejudice to the work that he was set on doing, now begin.

His way took him through the church-yard, and when he was there he hesitated for a few moments by the side of the open grave which contained his treasure, and which he meant to carry off before the morn-ing. But at that present he had something else to do; and as he thought of what it was he struck away below the church to-wards the tarn. The waters were already close to the churchyard—which sloped in the direction of the church—and by morn-ing, from the ceaseless flow of the mountain torrents, they would probably be washing near to some of the tombs.

The tarn of Black Moss, which flowed into a stream on the which there was a bobbin mill, had gates such as are common to the country. In times of long drought, times scarcely ever known in either West-moreland or Cumberland, these gates were open, so that the flow to the mill below

might, even in the driest seasons, never
cease. The tarn, from the many mountain
runners which came into it, hardly, however,
ever fell below a certain level, and had never
been known to be dry. Indeed, like many
of the tarns in Cumberland, it was very deep
in some places, and from the exceeding cold-
ness of the water near one of its shores, it
was said in the valley that just there it never
had been bottomed. But after heavy rains
the tarn had sometimes been unmanageable.
Once within the last five and twenty years,
when a very rapid ground thaw followed
upon weeks of snow, the waters had over-
flowed, and the valley round was for a long
time under water; some of the statesmen
had been very heavy losers, and some of the
sheep farmers had been sorely visited. For
miles below the mill the stream was full of
the sheep which had been swept away.
Here and there a cottage was knocked down,
and many, to escape from the waters, deserted
their houses. The tarn had at that time
threateningly surrounded the vicarage to a
depth of many feet, covered the churchyard,

and poured into the church itself, so that
some lives were likely to have been lost, and
certain of the head-stones to have been overset. The vicar had been carried out of a
top window by one of his flock, who fetched
him away in a boat; and then, at a meeting
held at the Fish Inn, it was resolved that
a new vicarage should be built on higher
ground. But when the water presently
abated, so did the fervour of the valley to
take their vicar out of his perils; and when,
in after years, Guy Melchior went there,
nothing had come out of the meeting at the
Fish. But as so many sheep were swept
away, it was considered a necessity to do
something to the tarn. And the sheep in
the valley were therefore of more account
than the shepherd in the vicarage. So there
was another meeting at the Fish, and
gates were ordered for the tarn, and for a
quarter of a century they had seemed sufficient
to check all such great disasters, although
the floods rose often very high. After heavy
rains these gates were eased, so that however
much the water behind might gather and press

on, yet it could not rise above them. There was always such an escape that mischief could scarcely follow. And Black Moss felt it had done wisely not to build another vicarage.

It was to these rudely fashioned gates that Gideon Cuyp, that evening, after leaving the churchyard, made his way. The old man who was charged with the keeping of the waters of the tarn was never abroad much after eight, therefore Cuyp believed there could be now no danger in the doing of the work that had to be done. He stood there looking wistfully about with this fixed and foul resolve. He meant to shut the gates, which then, because of the flood, were eased, so that the water behind them, as it presently rose and was kept back, might sweep the country. It would, he well knew, so continue to rise and spread, until at the last it would pour over the gates; but it would not after that sort get free before, as he concluded, it would have done that to the priest which he was minded it should do. The water, as it rose, would first surround the vicarage, for the vicarage lay lower than all other houses in the valley, and was the nearest to the tarn. Long before the morning broke, it would so have risen that, at first trickling into that lower room in little drops, it would begin to reach the bed, until it overtook Guy Melchior as he lay there in his sleep. The undertaker knew that this had nearly happened to another vicar once before; but this would not be nearly; this he meant should happen, and should not miscarry. So Cuyp went to the gates assured that this night's work would never need to be repeated. He did not think the vicar could escape, even if the water did awaken him before he should have fallen asleep for ever. Guy Melchior could not reach an upper room without facing the water that would burst upon him if he should try to get upstairs; because to get up there he must first go through his little parlour. And fine swimmer though Cuyp knew the vicar was, he did not think that any swimmer could prevail in that night's flood, therefore the undertaker was not fearful that Guy Melchior could be saved by getting through his window.

Gideon Cuyp had already ascertained, as has been seen, that the vicar was not now sleeping on an upper floor, and it seemed to him, from the calculations he had made, that by midnight, or sooner, there must be many feet of water in Guy Melchior's room, stealing up the bed, and encompassing it, and over the young life that was lying there. And to the end that there might be nothing to hinder the progress and consummation of this thing, Gideon Cuyp purposed, after he should presently have secured his gold, to return to the vicarage before the waters should have come about it ; and if the casement of the vicar's room was closed, noiselessly to set it open.

A little after ten he had shut the gates and locked up the water of the tarn. That which he had been minded he should do was done now. Anyhow there would be for ever blood upon his soul, in deed or in intention, let the issue of his terrible contriving be what it might. There was only

this thing more—to cast the boat adrift
upon the tarn so that there might be no
escape, even if there should chance to be a
cry; and as he pushed it from the shore
into the mists, he drew his outside coat
closer about him, and limped back towards
the open grave.

The waters, when he got there, were
coming on apace. Foot by foot they were
creeping up nearer and nearer to Cuyp's
prey. Through the mist, the moon and the
stars could just be seen; but for all these
lights the night was beginning to grow
darker and darker. There was no one
stirring, as it seemed to him, as he leaned
upon his shovel; no one stirring to tell to
the valley of the flood that was coming. It
would be, he reckoned, full three hours
yet before those gathering waters should
eddy round the vicar's bed; therefore he
would first dig up his gold before he need
go to set Guy Melchior's casement open.
The rain and the wind had ceased since
noon, and before he went down into the
grave he could see, although the darkness

grew, that the mists above the tarn were beginning to lift and shut out the stars. And then he waited to see the lights in the cottages going out one by one; the waters would not come round those who were resting there until they should be deep in the lower rooms of the vicarage. The eager tarn had already reached the churchyard wall, and was almost rippling against the gate; and Gideon Cuyp looked over to watch it trickling down towards the vicar's house. Then he heard at a distance the voices of those who had come together at the Fish. A shout, and then a groan, and then the sound of many voices, as it seemed to him, struggling in hot contention. He was almost sure he heard Job Redcar louder than the rest; but then he knew the swiller must be on his bed; so he thought that he would get into the pit and deliver his treasure from the grave.

"I'd like varra weel ta be makin' 'em droonk this neet messel; they are a gae bit bettre waar the' are, gettin' beered oop yonder; if they waar aboot, it's likely

they wud mel* er me, an' be hinderin' me er
doin' this job," said Cuyp, who was now
assured he should succeed, as he went again
towards his gold. "I sall for ivver ha'
teem ta mak' an end er this job a deal
afoore watre's oop, an' get away yonder
ta th' vicar's, joost ta mak' his weendow
snoog."† And as he muttered this he
turned to where all the thoughts which
he could spare from his gold were centred.
There was a light in one of the windows of
the vicarage, and it was easy to see Guy
Melchior's shadow on the blind. Cuyp
crept along beneath the churchyard wall,
that he might the better watch the move-
ments of the vicar. He could hear the
cough; he could see Guy Melchior take up
his Bible to read, as was his wont before he
went to bed. And then could Cuyp see the
doomed man kneel down by his little bed
and pray.

"It's likely aboot th' last teem, I's
thinkin', that he'll be doin' ov yon gae treek,"
said the undertaker, as he took himself to

* Meddle. † Window snug.

K 2

the work he had to do. The vicar, after that he had so prayed, came to the window and looked out. The mists were now so thick that he could not at all see how near the waters were by that time to him. And then the casements were closed, until Gideon Cuyp should open them again. After watching for a while the vicar's light went out, and the undertaker, making very sure he was not watched, got down into the grave in the which he had hidden his golden loves. Then Cuyp fell to work upon the clay. He believed that he could raise his chest of gold within an hour; and then as he carried it along he could very gently set the vicar's casement open.

Now it had never once entered into his mind that he should not find his gold where he had put it. Had he not watched the mound which covered .it, and the long line whereon the daisies, grew and had he not seen that it never had been touched? And then no man suspected him of having anything to hide. Such as he had, and such as he had gotten, it was believed he spent ; therefore he would not have been followed when he buried this.

And then Gideon Cuyp was also very sure that one so nearly silly as was Sawrey Knotts, would never play him false ; but still, he did not like what had been spoken by the sexton in the morning about hidden treasure in these places ; and he bethought him he would just cast his eyes up and down the golden rows before he came out of the grave that night.

The planks on which the mourners were to stand round the pit's mouth on the morrow, were already distributed about the grave. Everything had been made ready by Sawrey Knotts for the burying away of the very last of a long line. There even stood a little cone of prepared dirt that was to represent the earth, and the ashes, and the dust, in the next day's sublime and awful ceremonial. By the side of these had laid the sexton's pick and shovel ; and taking these in one hand, with a lanthorn in the other, Gideon Cuyp noiselessly and gently had let himself down. And he worked on, for the clay was heavy with the rain that had fallen upon it in the early morning ; and time went by, and Cuyp had not got out his gold.

When first he put the lanthorn down, it then had seemed to him as if big drops were falling on him from above ; but he did not set himself to think what they could be. Now he was not sure but that he had better get on to the top, and go and do that to the vicar's casement, for it had some time gone eleven. Once he had cast his shovel down and was half way up ; but, because of the love he bore his gold, he dropped anxiously back into the pit again. It might be he was watched ; and if he left it now, some thief would likely come and steal it away. So Cuyp wiped his brow, and girded up his loins, and resolved that he would not cheaply sell his life if any thief should come. The night was now very hot, and there was thunder in the air.

"It'll evven tak' ma a gae bit langer,*" said Cuyp, as he dipped about upon the clay. "I'll joost be seein' hoo th' wattre is coomin' on—

* Longer.

nae, nae, bet I'll be gettin' quit ov' this lile
job;" and so he stopped and toiled on until
he came upon the chest in the which he had
some time before committed his soul to the
ground—for never was the soul of Gideon
Cuyp parted from the goodly company of
unsweated sovereigns. And then he scraped
away the clay, afterwards, in his great joy, performing certain fantastic steps upon the lid.

He did not think about the vicar now. He
did not think that the waters he had so locked
up were stretching through the churchyard
grass. He sat him down upon his gold,
and apostrophized it, and seemed as though
he could caress and take into his arms the
chest in the which it lay. To him it was not
possible to turn away even in that hour,
when it was likely to be so very ill for
him to stay, from looking into the great heap,
to feel, to clutch, to count, to hold up to the
moon's light the golden rows that he had
once piled up, and which, from then even
until the present exhuming, he had never
in the spirit left. He thought that he could
wait until he got it home; but then, whilst

he was minded to carry it away, he felt it was too dear not to be looked upon without any further putting off; so he resolved he would not put it off.

Gideon Cuyp had, indeed, often felt, when it was buried there, that it tore his heart to leave it in the clay. But he had at such times consoled himself when the thought was strong upon him that he would tear it up and have it nearer to his hands, to his eyes, to his heart, where its violation should be impossible, even if it chanced to be discovered; and then he was also much consoled by the belief that the secret of his having gained so much gold was but very little likely to get beyond him. Yet he could not now persuade himself to carry it to his home without counting it over and seeing if a piece were missing. He did not think of the vicar's casement, or of the vicar's doom; he did not think of the half a million of money, and the thousand pounds a-day that had been scorned by Minna Norman. He had not then a thought for anything but that which was buried in that pit. And the wind sighed in the old yew close by, and he did not hear the coming of the waters as they crept by the graves.

Full of these thoughts concerning his meeting with his loves, he leaned back, every now and then a little eager cry escaping from him, against the deep clay walls. Then stooping down over the chest, by the application of some secret process, the lid with a spring started back.

" Me pretty yans, me conny yans, ye be gae breet* an' bonny; weel, weel, I's nit geean ta be lettin' ya stop by yerssels; ya sall coom thy ways wimma, ye sall coom thy ways." And he chuckled, and with rapture felt certain of the pieces, and called them " Me looves, me darlin's," and was otherwise familiar.

When he had presently mastered some of the emotions that at the first meeting over-came him—when he had fondly talked to, and with ravishing tenderness had apostrophized the layers, he proceeded carefully to count each coin, until he could persuade himself

* Bright.

that not a piece was missing. He might so have persuaded himself when the lid had started back, for then it could be seen that not a piece had been disturbed: but then Gideon Cuyp liked to be very certain of his loves.

And now he was fully persuaded that nothing had been filched away; he had fingered every one; and when he found his loves were faithful he made a little caper in the pit. Then he shut them down and lifted up the whole, to hug and fondle the only thing he thought had ever been constant to him. He did not think how close had clung another. He did not think of Minna Norman. In the presence of his golden loves he did not think of her who had said to half a million, I do not desire you, and to a thousand a-day, I would the rather have one hundred pounds a-year. And then he clutched up his chest that he might get out of that grave.

"Coom its ways, coom its ways," he said, as though it were a thing of life, as he tried to lift it up.

When these transports were beginning to abate, he stayed awhile to listen before he got out on the top, lest there might be those about to watch him. And then it was it seemed to him as though he heard the sounds of voices coming nearer and nearer, and the voice of the swiller far above them all. And he felt as though his blood would freeze when he heard what the swiller's voice was urging—" Tak' he ta th' tarn; ta th' tarn wi' Gideon Cuyp!" Was it that these sounds were begotten of his fancy; or was it that Job Redcar had slipped off his death-bed to be avenged of that coat? And then fainter and fainter got the voices, and Gideon Cuyp was set on persuading himself that he had been mocked by his own heart's dread, and that of a truth Job Redcar was not out to seek him. But still he could not get to be himself again. "Ta th' tarn wi' Gideon Cuyp!" was ringing in his ears, and the blood of the affrighted wretch still went on curdling. And then it came into his mind, had he been seen to touch those gates to shut the waters up? Was he to be cast

into the tarn that he had made so full?
And lest the pale reflection of his light
should by any chance bring violent hands
about him, he put out his lanthorn, held his
breath, and listened. There was nothing
stirring—there was in that grave no sound
but the loud beating of his craven heart.
And then, as his abject terrors almost made
him cry aloud, he bethought him, " Because I
am old they will spare me, they will not,
drown me like a dog. And many will plead
for me, and I shall be taken out of the
waters, even if I am cast into them ; for will
not the memory of the many excellent and
devoted things that I have done be strong
to save me ?" And then he stood up again,
and listened, but there was nothing —
nothing but what was like to the music of
the earth when the ground is soddened ; and
this, too, had the seeming of coming nearer
and nearer. Then the clay broke from the
sides, and rattled heavily upon his feet ; and
after that there was again a fall of something
that had weight, and that had also life. He
felt his flesh would creep when it came into

his mind what this moving thing must be—
the voices he had heard, and which had died
away, had not returned, therefore he was
purposed to get up out of that grave. All
above was still, only that there was, he
thought, a soaking sound amongst the grass.
So again he struck a light, and followed with
his eyes the flickering and dim reflection
round the pit—then he could see how
much too long he had stayed to toy there
with his gold. At one side just above his
head there was an opening from which the
clay was continuing to drop, whilst the face
of one rat and then of another crowding to
the mouth of the opening, showed to him
what they were which were swarming in that
hole. Those of them that were already in
the grave in the which he was standing,
now ran round and round, over his feet, and
about his chest, with a great noise, until he
tried to recollect something concerning
those who had been eaten of these things.
But he could also see that they scarcely
noticed him, and were the rather trying to
escape up the slippery walls. So that it

seemed to Gideon Cuyp that they were
striving to avoid him and were in too great
terror on their own account to turn upon
him. Lifting himself up to reach the top,
for now he knew how greatly it concerned
him to be getting from that place, he saw
that water was driving out the vermin, and
was fast oozing from the hole the rats had
made. He also knew that heavy drops were
falling on him from above, and heavier and
heavier they came, until it seemed to be a
stream that was upon him. Then he knew
that he was lost; then, for an instant he
thought with the horror of despair of the
rising waters of the tarn—of the tarn that
his own hands had made to rise—then he
knew what brought these rats upon him;
they had seen the waters and were fleeing
from them, and Cuyp, as he impotently
tried to wrestle with his awful doom, cried
unto men and unto God to save him. As he
clutched at the rope, by which he had come
down, and would have swung himself up,
the earth that was round him heaved, and
groaned, and bulged, and cast him back.

And then the flood of his own contriving was on him and over him. A choking and appalling cry of stifled agony broke from the drowning and climbing wretch; whilst he clutched with gurgling oaths the slippery sides as they pressed closer and closer in upon him.

But he had ordered the style of his own burial, and his own rats were the only mourners. The tarn in its progress had broken into the churchyard drain, driving the rats before it; and now as it swept across the tombs, there was nothing to be seen but its eddies curling round the crosses and the stones, and the breath-bubbles coming up out of one of the graves.

CHAPTER V.

ON THE TRACK.

WHEN Job Redcar, and those others who were with him, after they left the house of Gideon Cuyp, had gone but a little way towards the church, they were met and driven back by the flood; the moon was almost shut out by the mists; and in the bewildering darkness some were already in the water. They had known that the tarn was high, but since the putting up of the gates the waters were scarcely ever out after this sort; therefore they were at their wit's end to conceive into what they had come; and it was not long before their confusion became general. They began to think that the old woman, knowing of this flood, had lied to them concerning the whereabouts of Gideon Cuyp, so that they might not take him; and many of them were for going back to force from her the truth as to where the undertaker had hidden himself. And some said that John Tibbs had been before them, and had instructed the woman how they should be hindered. But it could not be agreed amongst them who had done this thing; and, meanwhile, the waters were driving them back the way by which they came. They were off the track of Gideon Cuyp now, and it was only after they had gone round by the great Ghyl, and had got on to the Raise of Black Moss, that they were at all able to agree amongst themselves how they should get upon the track again. Through the darkness they were just able to see how the waters had occupied the valley, and how that they would soon be reaching to their own cottages; and each one for himself began to think that it were better to let Cuyp go than that this flood should be coming upon all that he had. Nevertheless, no one would take the first step back, and the swiller seeing how it was, asked of them bitterly if they were afraid " er a lile soop ov wattre ?"

"Nae, Job, it isn't likely," said one who had passed nearly all his days in one of the lead mines of Red Moss, and of whom it was reported that he did not know what fear might mean. "Nae, nae, a care nowt for what's parlish,* a promus ya."

"Varra weel, girt John, then wyah is ya flate ta be coomin' on?"

"Bet a isn't flate, Job, ni' flackering† neither. I's thinking, varra sendry,‡ I's ne meear flate er wattre than thine ain steg.§ Nae, nae, a isn't flaayed‖ aboot messel, Job, bet I's aboot t'aald wife; a gae lock's likely ta be gettin' drooned."

"It canna be risen, Job, a gae deal meear, an' wives won't be takkin harm if they'll be mindin' th' sneck,¶ an' will na becoomin' oot. It'll ha doon awe macks** er mees-chief be noo 'll this fleeud; bet it'll likely be a way

---

* A Westmoreland word signifying dangerous, and the miner was a Westmoreland man.

† Frightened. ‡ Different. § Gander.
‖ Alarmed. ¶ Latch. ** Sorts.

er mindin'; it's bin risin' at a terble speed, it has, hawivver."

"Ay, ay," said another, "it's mebbie agin th' parson's door be noo."

"Hey, mon, bet it'll ha gloppened* he a bit: it'll ha meeak'd he ta glooar† a deal," said the miner; "I'd leever‡ it waar messel as he. I's quite er opeenion this job hasn't bin doon graaidly.§ I'll warr'n oos it's th' treek er soom gae rappis‖; th' tarn hasn't bin er this way for deal er years. I's sure it's th' job er a ragabrash,¶ a is that."

"Bet, me lads, he'll be gettin' o'er head weel t' parson if we don't kip stirrin'," put in Job Redcar, anxiously.

"Ya canna geean at wattre," said Sawrey Knotts.

"Hod thy din, Sawrey, thou'rt boggled** an' a maislikin,††" roared the huge miner; "we's bawn‡‡ if ye isn't."

"An' a can tak' ya yander, if ya be minded ta clim',"§§ said Job.

* Surprised.	† Stare.	‡ Rather.
§ Honestly.	‖ Scoundrel.	¶ Bad Man.
** Afraid.	†† Foolish fellow.	‡‡ Going.
	§§ Climb.	

"Ay, ay, we's climmers; gie es yar gaapen,* Sawrey, we'll ha ni foin-awt;† gie es thy kneeaf,‡ mon." So Sawrey Knotts and big John were after this sort reconciled; and they all followed Job along the Raise, by taking which course they were the better able to avoid the water until they should be close upon the vicarage.

"It's evven as slape§ as slape, it is sooa," said Sawrey Knotts, struggling for foothold, as they stood on the slanting summit of the Raise.

"An' there's nowt ta click‖at; I's deg'd¶ wi deet**—I's bettre doft,"†† cried out the miner, as he rolled over in the dirt; "bet a bethinks ma a heard soom fooak coo‡‡ oot."

"Ay, John, a bethinks ma it's th' parson shoutin'; he'll be gettin' drooned—coom, me lads, let's away," urged Job Redcar, and they poured down the slope towards the vicarage.

There was a light in the upper room; and, as well as could be seen, the waters

---

* Hands.   † Quarrelling.   ‡ Fist.
§ Slippery.   ‖ Snatch.   ¶ Covered.
.** Dirt.   †† Undrest.   ‡‡ Call.

were filling the lower rooms as they broke in at the casements.

"They's wick,* hawivver," said Sawrey Knotts; "t' parson, an' aald ooman."

"Titter oop coed· tudder oop;† they's nit smoard,‡ I'll warr'n es," said the miner.

"There's bin a sad set meeak'd on it," put in Job.

"That's trew, Job; we's bin nigh enoo sleeveless arrant;§ we's joost in teem ta sarra‖ he, puir mon," replied the miner.

"It's geean doon is wattre," said the sexton.

"Ay, it's faron;¶ it wor roond yon bor-terry** a bit. sen," said the miner.

By this time they were near enough to the vicarage to make themselves heard, and as near as they could go for the flood.

"Gie a girt shout, me lads," said Redcar from the front of them; and the shout was given with a will, and the vicar opened the casement of an upper room.

---

* Alive.   † The first up awoke the other.
‡ Smothered.   § Going to no purpose.
‖ Serve.   ¶ Fallen.   ** Elder tree.

"Munea* coom ta ya," roared the miner. "I isn't flaay'd wi' th' wattre—sall a fetch ya a stee,† Meester Melchior?"

"I'm safe, my friends, thank God," said the vicar. "I shall take no harm if the waters do not continue to rise; but I am afraid there is some one about who has been overtaken. A cry awoke me just now that seemed to come from the churchyard; and when I looked out I found the water almost in my room."

"There's likely summut ta dae wi' th' gaates," said one, "bet this terble girt soop 'll be o'er 'em be noo."

"Wesn't vicar teltin' es as hoo he heard fooak aboot as mooad‡ or greaan'd?"§ inquired big John.

"Ay, John, an' we'll be startin' ta fint 'em; it's a gae mash oop, it is, hawivver," said Job Redcar, "an' it fairly caps ma hoo it coomd aboot."

"Leave me, my good men," said the vicar. "You see I shall not take any harm,

---

* Must I.   † Ladder.   ‡ Shouted.
§ Groaned.

and there are others who may be wanting
your help. If it comes to the worst, I can
swim for it. Just see if there be not some
one who may be in trouble up yonder in the
churchyard."

And the vicar heard the sounds of their
voices dying away. But after that they
had left speaking to the vicar, there were
many stragglers who rolled down the
slippery bank of the Raise into the water,
only—with great indifference as to that
which had happened to them — to pick
themselves up again, till, in the end,
they nearly all were drenched, but none dis-
heartened.

As they got nearer to the churchyard,
because of the increasing depth of the water
over its slopes, they at once saw that it must
be many hours before they could possibly reach
to it. And so did they all keep watch, not one
of them fell away, between the vicarage and
the graveyard until the day should break, and
could see in which direction they might the
best offer their services. A little after midnight the water had begun to fall; therefore

they knew that their homes would not be perilled.

The scene at the gates at dawn was such as no one even in that valley had probably ever seen before. The waters from the tarn were pouring over the gates, whilst the stream below was swollen to many times its natural size. It was said of Black Moss that its ghyl was a thing to see. But never had that ghyl been so grand to look upon as was now the torrent which was sweeping from the tarn. The low lying lands that the stream went through were now a sheet of water, and some of the flocks in the pastures had been terribly thinned. As it presently began to get lighter little patches of land were seen to be fast cropping up in the sea of waters. Those who all that night through had expected to be instantly surrounded, were now running out to see how it had fared with those of their neighbours whose cottages were nearer to the tarn; and by when the sun was fully up they were all crowding round towards the gates. But they had none of them forgotten the vicar—

they knew the vicarage would be the first house in Black Moss to be in danger—and until it had been told that Guy Melchior was safe, many had learnt of his escape from his own lips.

It was early seen that the disaster had been wholly precipitated by the shutting of the gates when there was a gathering flood behind, and with every beck, and ghyl, and runner swelling the area of the waters. Therefore it at one time did not seem to be going well for the old man whose business it was to work these gates; and he could with difficulty persuade those who had come together, and who were mostly in a hasty mood, that he had left them open over night.

" That's varra weel ta bethink ya ta be sayin' this, David; bet wo's* bin at gaates ? it's ni goode ta be greetin ;† tell hoos‡ that."

" Gaats waar oppen when a geeand ta ma bed—this treek waar doon at neet."

" When was't oonder roogs§ last neet, David ?"

---

* Who's.   † Crying.   ‡ Us.   § Bedclothes.

"Mebbee be eight, happen afoore."

"That's trew," said one who was looking on; "a waar here messel, an' a cud discern a lile glimmer in David's room, an' a knaa gaates wor oppen then."

So after this it was not then considered necessary further to question the old man of the gates. Then the people began to ask of one another what it all could mean; and some muttered, and others whispered, and said there was malice or worse in it, and that they would "bottom it oop."

As soon as the waters had gone down from the vicarage, Job Redcar and the rest went back to Guy Melchior to report the empty result of their search in the church-yard. Everything—so at least Sawrey Knotts the sexton said—was much as he had left it there the day before; only the grave he had been digging was full of water, and his pick and shovel seemed to have been washed into it, for they were not to be found.

"The water must all out by twelve o'clock for the funeral—you'll not forget that, Sawrey?"

"I isn't likely ta be behint wi' it; a hasn't sick a madlin,* I'll warrn yer, Meester Melchior."

"Very well, Sawrey, I shall look to you ;" and then turning to Job Redcar, the vicar asked, "Have you heard if there has been any accident through last night's disaster ?"

"There's a deal er beeasts be dead," said the miner, "an' I've heard telt that slape Toomas Staveley's girt teap'st bin drooned."

"Ay, ay, Job, bet Meester Melchior's meanin' if owt er fooaks bin droon. d ; we hevn't heard tell er nin ; bet Gideon Cuyp hesn't bin heeam ivver sen last neet."

"Mr. Cuyp not been home since last night ?" repeated the vicar, with some surprise and anxiety. "Why, he was only here last evening."

"By gin, exing yer pardon, Meester Melchior, bet it's evven he, it's evven Gideon Cuyp es ha doon this gae treek," shouted Job Redcar, as he almost capered round the astonished vicar ; " he knaas we is questin he, an' he kips hissel away."

* Bad memory. † Ram.

"Come, come, Job, I cannot permit you to say such things. Do you know that you are accusing of a very serious crime a man who is not here to answer for himself; who has always borne the highest character amongst us; against whom there never was the breath of a *just* suspicion?"

And the vicar felt the better for this little speech on behalf of Cuyp, for he did not doubt but that he had greatly wronged the undertaker. And he looked very seriously at Job, and said, "You must forget yourself, Job Redcar, to wrong so good a man."

"Nae, nae, bet a dusn't, Meester Melchior. It's a serious ploomp wrong a tak' it that's o'er girt to be trew er Cuyp. I's meanin' what a ses, Meester Melchior—"

"Then I will not hear another word you have to say, Job."

"We waar oot ta quest, an' tak he, Meester Melchior, for th' fever job," put in the miner who was called big John; "and noo he's bin at this sad set. He's a serious dannet ta sarra es thissen."*

* He's a very bad man to serve us in this way.

"What do you mean by this, John, and you, Job, and you all?" asked the vicar, looking upon them with great displeasure.

"Why joost this, Meester Melchior, an' ne meear," answered. Job Redcar, coming up near to speak; "joost this, that Gideon Cuyp hissel contrived ta kip th' fever ameeang es, ta kip it stirrin' aboot oop an' doon, first that yan sud tak' it an' then todder*; an' when we's coomd, me an' Sawrey, an' big John yonder, an' a deal er es ta fint he, he's a gae skoolker, he's crappened† away: that's what we's meeanin', Meester Melchior, an' we isn't geean ta loss he."

"Nae, nae, that's trew," put in the great miner, "that's for evver trew; we'll evven rive he ta bits, the gae filth."‡

Almost staggered by the terrible things that he heard, Guy Melchior sought to lead those men away to something else. But they would none of them be so led; they would not be so balked. They were off the track, but they meant to be on

* Another.   † Crept.   ‡ Scoundrel.

it again ; and Job Redcar went back to the
business of the undertaker's visit to the
vicarage, and said he was persuaded Cuyp
meant ill by coming there.

"Now, just to convince you, Job, how
much,.and how grievously you wrong Mr.
Cuyp, I'll tell you that he was only here last
night out of kindness to me. He thought
that he could serve my interests, and therefore he came. Does this convince you how
wickedly you have spoken ? He——"

"Nay it doosn't, Meester Melchior. I's
nowt bet a plaan mon, an' that's trew.
He's a saft yan is Cuyp, he is that ; for
ivver a hypocriting," interposed Job Redcar ;
but the vicar without heeding the interrup-
tion went on—

"He came with some friendly words to
me from Mr. Massareene, the minister who
is staying at the Abbey, and, in his concern
for my well-doing, to inquire about my
cough, and to suggest that I might find it
to my advantage to sleep downstairs until
my health is better."

And the vicar as he said this concerning

Cuyp'scoming, turned pale and sick at the terrible thought that was upon him. He felt that that which now covered his face must supply a fearful commentary upon some yet unspoken words. And he said he was a little faint, and asked that they would open the casement, and then he went on again.

"Mr. Cuyp also expressed a fear that if the matter was not looked to, the tarn would be round here some night, and that then —then I might have to—to—swim for it." And now he felt sicker than he felt before, and called to the old woman to bring him a little water.

But Job Redcar when he heard the words leaped up, and was otherwise demonstrative. "We's reet, John, we's reet, Sawrey. It's evven as a bethowt ma it waar; it waar Gideon Cuyp wo shoot them gaates. Th' tarn's a deal o'er coomfortable for sick a marpy."

"Ay, ay, it's evven he," sobbed out the big miner, "wo's taard* me oonspaand† barn frae ma, when th'lile tinny yan waar grepen‡

* Who's torn.   † Unweaned.   * Clasped.

in me ain arms; a canna bide th' thowt, a canna bide it."

"Tak' oop, John, tak' oop, we'll ha' he at tarn, a promus ye."

"Bet that weel nit gimma bock ma bonny lile yan, or meeak ma nit sooa dowly."*

Guy Melchior, as he heard these things which were spoken, could not himself have now resisted, or put from him the conviction that the guilt of the undertaker would yet be brought home. The suspicion of those who were before him was wild enough; but when Guy Melchior thought about that coat he knew within him that Gideon Cuyp *had* done this thing; yet did he shrink from letting it appear before those roused and maddened men—before those men who were already threatening Cuyp with various kinds of deaths.

"If it be so, my friends, if Mr. Cuyp is all that you say of him, we are not his judges—much less are we his executioners. You are accusing him of crime; and yet

* Lonely.

you do not hesitate to say that you will take away his life. Recollect this, that all may be explained; you are hurrying to the conclusion of his guilt upon that which is scarcely more than · a suspicion. Surely, Mr. Cuyp, of all men, has the least deserved this at your hands."

" I knaa ye'll mappen flite* ma, Meester Melchior," very quietly and firmly put in big John, " bet a canna help it. Gideon Cuyp waar at th' berrin† er ma conny barn, an' I'll joost noo be at berrin er Gideon Cuyp. I'll put he at tarn messel if I can click he ; an' I'll clod‡ he in joost waar it's a gae bit o'er brant§ for he ta crappen oot agin. He's for ivver fause.‖ Bet, I's thinkin' he'll ha diddert¶ afoar I's doon wi' he. He isn't sooa sackless** an' sooa swaymas†† as ye's believin'. "

And when he had so spoken, the big miner got up, with his teeth set, gave a great lurch, and went out of the vicarage.

---

* Scold.　　† Funeral.　　‡ Throw.
§ Steep.　　‖ Treacherous.　　¶ Trembled.
　　** Innocent.　　†† Shy.

Truly, the iron had entered into his soul.

The vicar was very angry, and said that he would have them punished for the violent things they threatened. Therefore Job saw that nothing would be gained by indicating too plainly what was to be the doom of Gideon Cuyp, and set to work to soothe Guy Melchior. Now the vicar had been minded that he would turn them out; but if they were set on killing Cuyp, he concluded it were better that he should get to learn their purpose that it so might be prevented.

"Nae, nae, Meester Melchior, we's sure ya knaas a deal mecar aboot th' goode Lord than hoos; bet we can mebbie bottom oop th' like er Gideon Cuyp. We's oot ta quest he, an' if we click he, we'll—we'll happen tak' he to th' joodge." And the swiller leered at his fellows as he said these words; for he thought that he could get the vicar off the scent.

"Then you would not touch or harm him yourselves, eh, Job?" asked Guy Melchior, searchingly.

Now Job Redcar could look no man in the face and tell a lie. If the apothecary had inquired about that beer, Job would have said that there were many bottles of it. The lusts of the·flesh were strong upon the ˇswiller; yet was he too true a man to tell a lie. And he looked full in the vicar's face and kept nothing back.

"Weel, weel, Meester Melchior, we's nowt bet plaan fooak; bet we telts trew; we canna bide lees, an' a isn't geean ta lee aboot Gideon Cuyp; a isn't a gae leear, is a, me lads?"

"Nae, ye isn't, Job," proclaimed many voices at once.

"I'm sure of that myself, Job," said the vicar.

"Varra weel then, as ya exes ma, I'll warrn es we is geean ta tooch Gideon Cuyp, an' that's trewth; we'll tooch he joost noo, a promus ya; we weel sooa, ch, me lads?" asked Job Redcar, looking round upon those eager men significantly.

Guy Melchior could see that nothing might be done by any appeal to their mercy;

they had manifestly come together to do to
the undertaker some grievous bodily harm ;
they vociferated that they would have him
in the tarn, and that they would drown him
as they would one of their own cur dogs
who was not cunning at sheep watching.
They were there to say that they would lay
violent hands upon him whenever they could
get to find him ; and though Guy Melchior
could not at all master the suspicion that
was now so strong again in his own mind—
for all that he was persuaded that Cuyp had
done this thing of which he was accused—
yet he was not the less resolved that the
undertaker should not be lynched by these,
his terrible accusers, but that he should be
otherwise judged.   So he set himself to
reason with those who said that they would
spill Cuyp's blood.

"Have any facts come to your knowledge
to warrant you in so accusing Mr. Cuyp,
my friends ?"

"Ay, a goode few," answered Job Redcar,
sulkily.

"Cuyp hasn't sick a girt loove ta yerssel,

Meester Melchior," put in Sawrey Knotts;
" a while sin' he waar keen agin ye, varra."

" An' ya knaa this yerssel, Sawrey?" inquired Job, turning round and facing the
sexton.

"Ay, ay, it's for ivver trew, Job; t' aald
body yonder telt ma, a while sen. 'Sawrey
Knotts,' ses she, 't' maister hesn't sick a
terble loove for t' vicar, he hesn't, hawivver.'
An' hoo d'ye coom ta knaa this?' ses I; 'a
ken it for why,' ses she, 'es a hears he at neets
meeakin a girt clatter, an' a taukin' oogly,
varra, agin Meester Melchior ta hissel, an'
sayin' es hoo Mees Minna yander sall na wed
he.'" And after Sawrey Knotts had been
delivered of this, he went back a little way,
wagging his head mysteriously.

The vicar felt that a cold sweat was standing on his skin, when he heard of his love
in the mouths of these rough men, but he
sat on, and those who were there did not
see how he was moved.

" It's enoo, an' meear than enoo, Sawrey;
coom, me lads, let's quest he; let's hev he at
tarn; ta t' tarn wi' Cuyp!"

"Stop, Job Redcar," said the vicar, standing in the doorway. "The first of you who lays a hand on Gideon Cuyp shall pass over my body. That which he may have done he shall answer for—but not to you— you shall none of you harm the old man." And he put on his hat and went his way to the undertaker's.

Job Redcar looked after the vicar, and it was easy to see that he was softened. "Me lads, t' vicar's reet, he's for ivver reet; he isn't like a gae lock* er parsons; let's gie o'er questin Cuyp; t' vicar ses t' aald rappis sall be joodged."

Now that the leader had given in, his followers were not for holding out. And in Black Moss there were none who set themselves against the vicar. Guy Melchior could have led them whithersoever he was minded. Therefore they would let Cuyp go.

"Weel, weel, Job, we's willun," said one, and then another. And the vicar went on to Cuyp's cottage, fearing greatly that the next doings of these men might be leaving them without the law.

* Lot.

"There's joost ta be gettin' quit er that soop er wattre at graave," said Sawrey Knotts, "an' then I'll be back agin." And when he had so said, he went down to the churchyard to get the water out of the grave, whilst his fellows went towards the gates, about which a multitude of people from most of the places round were now assembled. The statesmen, and shepherds, and miners, were gathered in a crowd together, some gesticulating, others seeking to stir up strife, whilst the greater part were listening open-mouthed, believing that the cause of so great a disaster was not a thing to be understood. But whilst certain of them were busied with surmises as to how the gates could have so got shut, others were occupied with the unaccountable disappearance, at such a time, of Gideon Cuyp. Many now came up to Job Redcar to inquire of him why he had not died; and others disposed themselves about the swiller to get the latest intelligence concerning this great flood; for Job was accounted to be in such matters of a deep understanding.

"An' I's glaad ta be seein' ye agin, a is, hawivver," he said, as he returned the grasp of the many hands held out to him. "It waar beer as deed it; or a suddn't ha' bin wick be noo."

"Nae, Job, thee lees; it worn't t' drink," screamed a woman, a total abstainer, who could not stand by and hear the praises of malt liquor. "It waar th' goode Lud— doesn't ye knaa it's a serious sin ta soop owt bet wattre."

"It waar th' goode Lud as gied me t' portre; an' I knaa we's telt in goode booke ta soop a lile wine for saak er hoos stomacks." And the total abstainer, who could not answer at all to that scripture, wrung her hands and cried, "Oh, oh, I's telt varra sendry* at meetin'."

"Bet wo's ben an' doon this treek wi t' gaates, Job?" asked another.

"Oh! it's wo's doon it ya'r exing? wyah, he as canna be fint; it's Gideon Cuyp."

They all fell back before the manner and style of the swiller's accusation. Some

* Different.

gaped, and some muttered, and many turned away from hearing what further things Job might have to say. At the last, one said, "He's evven droonk."

"Ay, ay," said the total abstainer, who now thought the time was come, and so struggled up to the front from the back of the crowd where she had hidden herself; "dudn't a telt ya he be beered oop?" and she almost screamed this out as she looked up and down upon their faces.

"Weel, weel, dry Bet, geean thy ways, we isn't at meetin'; ya cud evven soop t' Gowd Arks in,* I's thinkin'," said one, leading the shrieking woman away.

"Ay, ay, them totelers† can evven soop what th' sea-nags‡ sails aboot on dry. It's cleean agin Godil,§ these coorses‖ agin owt bet wattre; there's ne sense in't," said another.

"An' a conny few er 'em soops a deal er beer an' spurrit at chance teems when they can soop it snoogly. They're gay fause,¶

---

* A piece of water in Cumberland.
  † Teetotallers.   ‡ Ships.   § God's-will.
     ‖ Curses.   ¶ False.

they are, hawivver. Bet I's thinkin' thee
isn't reet, Job, aboot Gideon Cuyp."

"Ay, wesn't he a sarvant er th' goode
Lud, an' a trew?" put in another.

"Wasn't he for ivver a teemin'* hot stoof
inta hoos ta feel hoos stoomacks?" added
another.

"Bet a tell ya it's he," said Job Redcar,
fiercely; "it waar he, th' gae marpy, wi' his
hypocritin', as kipt th' fever ameeang es."

But few cared to listen; and Job Redcar
got no converts there to his suspicion.

"It isn't this wrong I'll be hearin' ya
doin' ta Gideon Cuyp for nowt, Job; if ya's a
mon ye'll feet,"† said one of the believers in
the undertaker, squaring up and pulling off
his jacket.

"Gie he thy kneaffs,* Job," said the
miner who was called big John, who had
then returned from looking after Gideon
Cuyp.

Nor was Job Redcar slow to strip, when
just as the two men were coming together,
Sawrey Knotts with but little breath left in

---

* Pouring. 　　† Fight. 　　‡ Fists.

him, and fewer words, rolled pale and inarticulate into the midst of them.

" What's t' dae wi' Sawrey?" asked the miner; " has't bin skreeng'd* till ther's ne bloode in ya; or has't got t'shakin'."†

But all that the sexton could do was to moan and point to the graveyard.

" Coom, coom, what ails thee, Sawrey?" persisted the miner; " thau leaks as if thau wor gaain ta greet;‡ thau er as white as aald wife's cap at aald wife hake."§

" Oh, oh !" at the last answered Sawrey. "Oh, oh! John, I's evven as seak as a peat.‖ I is, hawivver. He's—he's lygin¶ at—at—bottom—yonder—ploomb** oop, he is sooa —at graave ; a wes mad an' swet for fear, an' durstunt say a word ; a think he wur chained to th' spot—I dae sooa, becose he dudn't stur, an' a turned as seak as a peat, an' spewd oa et ivver wes imma.†† Oh, wons,‡‡

---

* Squeezed.   † The ague.   ‡ Cry.
§ Old woman's tea-meeting.
‖ A Cumberland expression to describe intense sickness.   ¶ Lying.
** Straight up.   †† In me.   ‡‡ Oh, dear.

I wes bad, a thowt a sud ha deed. Oh, oh! I isn't noo messel."

"Wo's lygin waar?"* asked Job Redcar, authoritatively.

"Why, Gideon Cuyp. Oh, wons, a thowt a sud ha deed."

"Tak' oop, tak' oop, Sawrey, ya's evven as white as drif,"† said the miner, kindly.

"Ploomb oop waar?" inquired one.

"Ploomb oop at graave."

"Dead! be he dead, Sawrey?" asked they all.

"Ay, dead enoo, if he isn't chained to th' spot."

And then they dragged Sawrey Knotts back to the graveyard, that he might show to them where Gideon Cuyp was lying.

The sexton had not by one word made the scene in that grave too ghastly or too horrible. Crushed with the clay that had fallen in on the undertaker, the stiffened arms held up, and the distorted features of the dead man's face, were only to be seen above the water — the hands clenched,

---

* Who's lying where.   † White as snow.

stretched up in his last awful agony, the eyes staring and set, his swollen tongue hanging from his mouth, and with every contortion of a terrible death, each one started back appalled as he came on to the brink of the grave.

" Th' dule's* gettan him, an' nact hoos," said the great miner with folded arms, as he alone looked down unscared.

" Bet he moosn't lyg here," said Job, preparing for action, and pulling off his jacket ; " he'll be corrooptin."

" Put this brat† on t' top er his face," said the miner. And then there were many offers to help Job Redcar and big John get up the body.

It soon began to spread from house to house that Gideon Cuyp had been found by Sawrey Knotts the sexton drowned in an open grave. Guy Melchior had been early on the spot; but then, the finding of the body was only the beginning of the mystery. When more of the water had been got out they came upon the open

* The Devil.　　† Cloth, or apron.

chest, for Cuyp when taken up was kneeling bruised and crushed upon his gold. Every one had some conjecture or speculation to offer that added nothing but to the general confusion. For had it not always been reported of Cuyp that he was poor? And none could account for this much lucre.

Under the directions of the vicar, they got the body and the treasure, on the which it was found, at once on the way to the undertaker's cottage, and there they were carried and set down.

The news had long before, even in the early morning, reached the Abbey that the waters had been out, and that Gideon Cuyp was missing; but it was nearly eleven before it came to be told that he was dead, and how he died.

Minna Norman had left the Abbey some hours before the telling of this, that she might herself get tidings of her uncle, and was even in Cuyp's cottage when the body and the gold were carried in.

"What's this, Mr. Melchior?" she cried out; "who are they bringing in here?" and

she turned her wild, pale face upon the vicar.
The suddenness of that which had come over
her had been more than she could bear; and
then the whole of that which was so true
upon that board, as it was set down by those
six big men, broke in on her, and she threw
herself upon the corpse and shook con-
vulsively.

Every eye was on her, and every eye was
moist with dew. At a sign from the vicar,
they all, noiselessly, went out, and Guy
Melchior gently led Minna away from the
body.

"Puir, puir lass, it meeak'd her whaker*
terble, it did sooa," said the miner, as he
shut the door. "I'll evven forgie her ooncle
if she exes ma, a weel, hawivver. I's cleean
fit ta greet messel." And big John did
rub his big hand across his eyes.

"He was loovin' enoo ta her, puir lass,"
said another as they moved away.

"She isn't si puir neether," added Job,
"if yon coopt be rank; wyah, mon, bet he

---

* Tremble, or shake.   † Chest, or box.

waar waxing* weel to do. She's a bonny yan an' a sweet."

And so did those men speak the praises of Minna Norman, till they were all dis-persed through their own homes.

After that they were gone, Minna Nor-man sat on for a little while ; and then she sighed a great sigh, and looked up, and she and the vicar left the cottage. They neither spoke as they walked along. They had neither spoken when they had been alone with the dead. Her bursting heart was too full of anguish for her to trust her new and withering sorrow to words; and Guy Mel-chior knew of a long experience, that in the morning of such a grief there can be no consolation. When they had, presently, reached the Abbey gates, he held out his hand. " God keep you—Miss —Minna in your great trouble," he said. She took his hand ; her bosom heaved faster and faster; she burst into tears; and then she was gone.

Minna Norman, of no bitter experience,

* Growing.

had never learnt that it may be expedient to search all hearts. And she had, ever since she could remember, loved the old man— whose cramped and disfigured body was only now a ghastly thing of lifeless clay—with sacred trust, and without one thought of suspicion. Her memory was full of kindly words, and of a face that in its ugliness had been never ugly to her. She had not heard of the many things that were now alleged against her uncle; of the deeds of blood which men said that he had done. And if she could have heard them all, her fresh, guileless heart would have told her that they must be false. They, who accused him, might have loaded his name with all the shapes of crime; but that would not have staggered her pure simple faith, or have poisoned her creed. She would not have believed this of him to-day, when the yesterday of her life was so warm with his love. The whirlwind of infamy had laid his memory low enough. But though the old tree was so utterly condemned, she would never come to look upon the trunk and

think the heart she knew those many years
could leave this rottenness in that which
was accounted but a heartless and a sapless
thing. She would not believe it, whoever
might bid her so to do; for, as yet, she did
not know there could be falseness in fond-
ness, and that a whole life might be a lie;
therefore was her sorrow more than she
could bear.

As Minna Norman was nearing the Abbey,
by that way in the which she once had
walked with Guy under those beeches, she
saw a woman making haste to come up
with her; and, presently, as the woman got
nearer, she could see that it was the same
who once before had come about a situation.

" My maid is remaining with me, if that
is what you come about," said Minna, hurrying on; and then bethinking her that she
might have seemed to speak harshly, she
added, " I am in very great trouble indeed,
my poor woman; but is there anything that
I can do to serve you?"

" I wor a gae bet yoonger messel, miss,
when me troobles coomd ta ma; it wasn't

that a wor pester'd* wi' a kerly-merly† er
a magget.‡ I's had a deal er girter trooble.
Bet a wud like ta spak wi' ya alean. I
isn't hoonger'd. I's vittuls enoo; it isn't
that, it isn't sooa."

"If you will tell me what you have to
say under these beeches, my good woman, we
are not likely I think to be disturbed."

."Bet, exing yer pardon, miss, there sud
na be chaance er that. I's gettin' summut
partic'lar as a moost tell yer."

Minna Norman did not know how to
answer to the importunities of the woman;
but in the midst of her own troubles she did
not wish to be to another harsh.

"Then, if you will follow me, we will go
where there shall be no listeners."

And the woman, following a little way
behind, they shortly afterwards reached the
Abbey, Minna leading the way into her own
room.

"I'm afraid I've only a few minutes I can
spare you this morning," she said, kindly,
as the woman, after they had reached the

* Worried.   † Trifle.   ‡ Whim.

room, still hesitated to speak that which she had to say.

"I's coomin' ta it joost noo, miss, a is, hawivver, bet a canna help greetin', ye are sick a gentle lady."

"No, no, I am not that; but are you tired, or ill, or unhappy?"

"It isn't that, a isn't that," the woman said, as she sank down upon her knees by Minna Norman's side. "Nae, nae, it isn't that, it's——"

But when she would have further spoken she was speechless.

CHAPTER VI.

JASPER TUDOR.

I⊤ was getting to be late on a bright, hot summer evening some years before the beginning of this history, that the coach from a considerable border town was setting dowu its passengers in front of the chief inn in Penrith. The landlord bustled out, for many and urgent were the calls for ale to wash out the dust; and the ostler fetched the steps, and with rough but successful gallantry got down two pair of ankles without any scandal.

"We sall evven be startin' agin in varra lile teem. We canna wait for nin," said the coachman, leaning over his already jaded horses. "Here's a gent for Pooley Brigg, Toomas," he added, turning to the landlord; "a gae stiff an' sharp yan an' awe; a dursn't speck ta he; a dursn't, hawivver;" and as the coachman spoke he pointed to a fair, well-looking man who had just got down from the box-seat.

"I'll manage he, I'll warr'n es, Jooan," said the landlord, who had some time concluded himself to be fit to treat with and deal with all tempers and all temperaments; and then the little man went blandly up to the stranger.

" Ya's stoppin' here, I's telt : can meeak ya varra coomfortable ; there isn't a bettre hoose than me's; there isn't, hawivver."

"You seem well able to recommend it," answered the stranger with a sneer; "the merits of a decent inn, I have heard, are best told by its customers," and he moved away; and the little, round, full-bodied landlord went after him.

" Like ta post it mappen ; we's a deal er goode nags ?"

"You seem to have the best of every-thing——"

"There's nowt ta bet es."

"You have said enough, man. I am,

worse luck, to learn of your fitness to keep
this hole. I shall want some supper and a
bed to-night; see that I get the one quickly,
and the other aired." And when the
stranger had said this he went into the
inn.

"Hey wons! he's terble lofty, an' carries
hissel' aboon ploomb,* he does, hawivver,"
said the landlord to the coachman.

"Ay, ay, Toomas, he's a reedent† mon,
varra; he wud flay‡ yan waar yan tae meet
he in a dowly spot; bet he's for ivver free
wi' his brass. I's gettan thissen," said the
coachman, tossing up a crown-piece.

"We'll blood he er them macks er things;
mebbie he's a Parlemen mon, an' them baits
yan anudther a deal."

"Noo, then, teem be oop," said the coachman, gathering up his reins: and then the
steps were brought, and the two pair of
ankles went up, and this time, perhaps, it
was not as it had been when they were com-

* This means that a person carries himself very
high.
  † Ill-tempered.   ‡ Frighten.

ing down, for there was a little scandal to the ostler and the helper.

"Seester* legs, Jooan?" said the helper; "they waar ploomp, varra. Ya shud hev coovered em oop a bit."

"Ay, ay, David, a happen shud; bet tha haed nice lile feet, an' it meeaks† ma think thae would pryuv‡ nimmel shipperts§ o'er oor brant fells." And as the ostler so delivered himself, the coach was rattling over the stones of the quiet town on its journey south.

After the traveller had presently had his supper, he rang the bell for the landlord, and Thomas Timmins, thus adjured, speedily presented himself, rubbing his stomach.

"Is your belly in flames with your own wine, man, that you so rub it?" asked the traveller; "I've been rubbing my own, but cannot put the fire out."

"I's rect enoo in ma stomack," said

---

* Did you see her.

† This word is sometimes pronounced maaks, and sometimes macks.

‡ Prove. § Nimble shepherds.

the little man, still chafing his protuber-
ance, "it's a gae goode stomack——"

" By ——! it must be if you put into it
that which you have sent up here for me to
put into mine. Look you, man, how can I
best get out of this infernal place to Pooley
Bridge ?"

" Why, there be evven a cooach tamorn,*
if ye be's ridin'," answered the landlord
meekly, and not appearing to heed his
visitor's disparaging and equivocal reference
to quite the first inn in Penrith; " bet
cooach joost noo isn't at awe to be deped on ;
there's a deal er coompany aboot oop an'
doon. A site er gents as coome here posts
it; it's a gae bit meear coomfortable.
There isn't sick anudther jarvy as a kips
for these jobs."

" You've *said* enough about the quality
of the things you keep, and I've also seen
and tasted enough; and take away your
hands from your stomach, man, or you'll
rub a hole in it. Are the roads as hard as
the rumps of your beasts, and as rough as

* To-morrow morning.

this cursed wine ? for I must be getting to
Patterdale by to-morrow evening, so send
me in something that isn't of your best by
way of change—for your best steak is stick-
ing in my chest this minute. And haven't
you got anything with a little less brandy,
for this is as hot as——"

"I's evven a gae wine rank wi' boddie that's
tied ta gloppen* ya; ya can hev it at eight
shillan, an' a gied ivvery fardon er foor poond
a doozen messel mappen foor year sen—a
deal er gent fooak hes sooped it here—Parlemen men an' sick like, an' they ses ta ma,
'Mr. Timmins, we nivver soopd sick wine
in oor lives, nivver.'"

"I can quite believe that, Mr. Timmins,
and I hope that I may never again. But
it must have cost you a lie or two, my friend,
between this and then, to give your mixture
such a history. I'll have no more of it; and
let me be called at six, for if your bed is at all
like to your board, my bones, I take it, will be
no better suited than has been my belly."

" Joost let ma bring ya anudther bottle—"

* Surprise.

"Not if you'd give it me. I've come out for my health, and I can't stand these experiments."

"Bet it's tied to kip ya wick; it's evven as goode for t' health as doctor stoof."

"And I dare say as vile. I want no doctor's stuff, my friend, unless that which you've given me already stops where it is."

"I's bethinkin' me a cud meeak it a lile less. Ye shall evven hev it for sivven shillins, ya sal, hawivver." And Thomas Timmins went away into his cellar; and the traveller was forced to taste a little, acknowledging it to be not quite so nauseous as the last.

The next morning, after an early breakfast, the incomparable jarvy stood before the inn.   .

"He isn't sick a coomly un," said the driver, seeing that the points of his horse were being criticized; "bet he's a deal er booan;* an' there isn't sick anudther climmer at coontry; there isn't, I'll promus ya."

"There's no mistake, at all events, about

* Bone.

the deal of bone ; there's some of it through here," said the traveller.

" He is thin, varra; bet, for awe, there isn't sick a feeder noowhere's."

" I dare say he enjoys what he gets, but would take a little more ; but if this is your best, there is no help for it." And then he went on to Pooley Bridge, the landlord not having failed to set down eight shillings for the historical wine, and otherwise to get substantial satisfaction for the many grievous reflections which had been cast upon the accommodation. And, in the end, everybody about the Inn had said that the stranger was "free wi' his toong an' wi' his brass."

At Pooley Bridge the traveller decided to walk on to Patterdale, then a straggling little village, lying at the high end of the Lake of Ullswater, and almost in the shadows of Helvellyn. In those days the hotels, which have since superseded with their magnificent appointments the homeliness that was then to be found in the country of the Lakes, had no existence.

Having turned aside at Ara Force, he was directed, after walking on another hour, to a little inn which seemed to promise such fare as he stood most in need of. He had come to fish the very considerable stream which runs through the valley into the Lake of Ullswater, and was only provided with such changes of clothes as he himself could carry. Having presently dined off broiled trout, and some delicious little cutlets of fell mutton, he bethought him he would see how the fish were rising, and went down to the water to cast in his flies. In those days the fishing in that stream was of the best; as good indeed as it is at the present in the adjacent Hawes Water, and Brothers Water. And to this day, when all the waters thereabouts are whipped so continually, Griesdale tarn, which lies immediately under Helvellyn, abounds with fish. But then there was no better trout stream in Westmoreland or Cumberland, than that which ran through Patterdale.

The fish on that evening rose greedily and eagerly at the traveller's flies about the time

of the setting of the sun, and with ten
brace in his basket, he went back to the
little inn, on the whole so well satisfied
with the sport which he had had, that he
was minded he would stay there some time
longer.

He was by the side of the stream next
morning before sunrise, and after repeating
the last night's performance, and somewhat
improving on it, was beginning to think that
he had well earned some breakfast, when a
strangely beautiful girl driving a cow before
her passed him, going in the direction of the
village. The fisher, who until then had
been concerned about nothing but his flies,
could not take his eyes from off her. The
morning had been soft, and the valley had
seemed very beautiful; but now came there
this simple loveliness, which was sur-
passing. Anything like to this in all his
experience of that which was fair he had
never seen. Dressed in the quaint and
picturesque costume of the country, her
golden hair, on which fell the slanting beams
of the risen sun, had escaped from beneath

the daintiest hat, falling wildly almost to her waist; and to such a waist as the fisher persuaded himself was not common to women. And she looked so maidenly and modest as she caught his glance and blushed, and not a whit less fresh even than that morning. He could scarcely believe he had not been some time looking on a vision. What was there in those cities or towns in the which he had lived that was beautiful like to this wild flower in this great garden? And then he thought, perhaps, that he would pluck off this flower, and bear it away with him into those cities and towns, and bear it as a man who looks with love upon a woman should? He also asked this of himself—but *then* he was not ready with his answer.

She had dropped to him with infinite grace the modestest curtsey as she passed; and then went on singing some tuneful snatches of a song to her cow, as she drove it before her up the valley.

The fisher stood like one fixed to the spot till the girl was out of sight, and then

cursing to himself his folly for letting her
pass without some befitting salute for that
intoxicatingly pretty curtsey, he hurriedly
put up his rod, stripped off his killing flies,
and went away after her.

Keeping at a little distance behind, he
determined to follow, and so discover where
she lived. And after again coming in sight
of her, and holding her in view, until she
presently reached the village with her cow,
he saw her stop before a cottage into which
she disappeared, her charge the while waiting
outside whisking her tail. The cow was
presently driven into a little back close by
an old man, and on the fisher getting to the
door he was able to see written over it these
words, " Noah Hermon's lodgings."

He had after the reading of this soon
made up his mind, that for very sufficient
reasons it would be better to lodge at Noah
Hermon's than at the inn. Accordingly
when he had breakfasted with such appetite
as remained to him after the vision that
had crossed him, he went out to see if he
could be at once received into the little
cottage.

The old man was at home, and with native honesty said that it was but a poor plain place; but if gentlemen could put up with that, he and his Daisy did their best to make them comfortable.

" I's nowt bet a plaan Westmorland mon messel, bet me Daisy's a tidy sort er lass, an' can dae varra ni owt—a isn't se soopple an' lysh as a waar a bit sen. I's gettin aald, a cud ni bide wi'oot me Daisy."

Therefore the terms were settled, and there was no difficulty about the fisher being taken in that same day as a lodger. So paying the reckoning at the inn, he came on at once to Noah Hermon's, and in the evening found himself to be in greatly improved quarters.

From the first, when he had seen the young girl in the early morning, lighted up with the fresh risen sun, he had begun to inquire of himself how she best might fall. He would tell her that he would hold to her and love her all his life through—that he would set her up—that she should be his mistress—a thing much coveted by many women—that she should have many horses instead of this one cow.. After this sort would he dazzle and encompass her; and this, too, is a sort of planning that goes on apace.

After so taking himself to Hermon's house, he said that he would have his tea, and he was well pleased to find that it was served by the beautiful one whom he believed was the same as was called by the old man Daisy.

"And what's your name, pretty one?" he asked; and the fisher, when he so willed it, had a voice that was pleasant in the ears of women—and he willed it now.

"I's cood* Edith, bet fadther coos ma Daisy; an' fadther ses a isn't pretty at awe, an' that a isn't ta be telt it."

"On my word, Daisy or Edith, which you will, they both are names that most excellently become you. So, so—Daisy, it has been told you before now that you are not altogether ugly—eh, pretty flower?"

"A isn't a flower—a's nowt bet a plaan

* Called.

lass es can meeak fadther stockin's, an' can dae spinnin' and knittin', an' for messel a goode calemanco gawn, an' a maunerly happron, an' sick like conny daisent things. A goode few as hev coomd hither ta feesh hev telt ma a isn't sa varra oogly; bet it's nowt tama what a is," she said, blushing and hesitating, and staying to hear no more.

Now the fisher was beginning to think that there might be here, after all, less of innocence than he had at the first concluded, and, if there were less, then he did not know that he should care to give to her his love. He would have her innocence or he would pass her by.

"By G—d! though, she's a very queen of girls;" and then he paced the little room restlessly until he almost fancied that he saw his nets close round her; and after this, as it was growing to be late, he thought it must be getting time to be going to his bed. Therefore he rang his bell for a candle, and she came in to answer to the ringing.

" Nay, nay—there is no such haste; stay awhile, Daisy—you will let me also call you

Daisy," he said, softly and gently, and his voice had in it those tones the which were so pleasant in the ears of women. "And now, startled one, tell me what to you is the old man Noah Hermon?"

"Sure bet he's fadther mine—me ain deary fadther."

"And where did you learn that pretty song you were singing to your cow this morning? I like it so well, that do you know I am going to ask you to teach it me."

"Weel, it's a sorry bit er song, bet it kips coo a bit quiet, though a doesn't knaa whaar a learnt it—mappen in Lunnon."

"And have you been to London, Daisy?"

"Ay, a's bin ta Lunnon—a has, hawivver; it wor last back end—wyah, a cud hev bin wed er Lunnon, I cud sooa, tul a mon et hed a girt shop, an' dond* as fine, an' leeak'd like t' aald squire here; bet a wud nit like ta leev in a tawn†—he wor me cusen's wife breeder‡—an' she meaad a girt tae due for ma tae hev he; bet a wadn't, I hed no mind at awe, a wor si teerd wi' waukin'

* Dressed. † Town. ‡ Brother.

threa mile i' th' streets — nae, a deal
warse than ivver a wor wi' a day's shearin';
me cusen* wa sa fat, she cud net wauk, soa
we maistly raaid, an' we olas† raaid at
coaches. Wyah, barn, yee may hev a coach
ea ony street; evvry soul ea Lunnon rides
ea coaches; hud up yer finger an' they'll
coom—they weel, hawivver; bet a must be
geeang; fadther's cooin' ma."

"And you shall go, singing bird, when
I've had a kiss," he said, trying to reach the
door before her; she, nevertheless, was too
quick for him, and was soon clear of his dis-
tasteful importunities.

All that night through did he lie awake
because of her, and it was not until morning
he began to assure himself that he had got
his traps about her. Then he got up before
the sun. Again he went to the stream—
again, as the sun got above the great Scar
did he meet her with her cow. All was the
same—only that she looked more beautiful
as she came over the fields with those pretty
bursts of bird-like song.

* Cousin.   † Always.

"You've bin stirrin' a bit," she said, as he
came up to where she was, for because of
his last night's importunities she had
been minded to pass through another
field.

"I have been long up at this stupid sport,
and I have been thinking. of you, Daisy;"
and he sprang up the bank to stop her.
"Nay, nay, I will not hurt you—I will not
harm you," he said, as he saw that she was
startled and seemed minded to leave her cow
and get away.

"Then if it's thinkin' ov ma ya's bin,
ya canna hae mitch ta bethink yerssel
aboot," she answered him, perhaps a little
archly.

"Yes, but then, Daisy, I can only forget
all else when I remember you. Come with
me, and I will love you, Daisy, better than
that old man yonder loves you; and I will
give you everything that you may ask to
have; and you shall ride in your own carriage, and have many horses instead of your
cow, and——"

"An' ya'll mappen loove ma till ye's seak

er ma; a gude few fooak has telt ma this afoore, an' fadther ses it wor a rappis* wor'd spak sooa tama."

"But you do not think that I would do you, Daisy, such a wrong; trust me, and come with me, my timid and my coy one. Come with me and be my own." And he would then have put his arms about her, had she not escaped him; and shaking her head quietly and reproachfully, she said, as she urged on her cow—

"Fadther telt ma they wasn't meanin' graaidly† wimma as wud spak tama sick as this."

"And the old man told you well, Daisy, when he spoke of others, but I will never harm or hurt you. Tell me now, have I the seeming of one who would do you any ill?"

"Weel, I canna think ya wud," she said, whilst the trust she felt from his softly spoken words sparkled in her lovely eyes, coming from behind the cow; " I's sure varra ya wud nit telt tama owt that wasn't trew."

* Scoundrel.   † Honestly.

"No, on my honour, Daisy, no; and now teach me the song."

And so they went along, and the cow switched her tail as Edith warbled that song; and the girl's young trust came fuller and fuller, until, at the last, she stedfastly believed in the fisher's words; for that voice which had music to so many women, had also music to her. And then he left her, after that it had been agreed that they should talk upon this matter further; and she went to the milking of her cow in the faith that he was not such a one as her father had spoken those hard things of. For had this one not said, "I will not harm or hurt you—no, on my *honour*, Daisy, no?"

So did they meet, so did her peril grow, for many mornings—for so many, that a month had presently gone by and he still stayed on; nearer and nearer was he getting to her heart—closer and closer was she coming to his nets. But he did not tell to her as yet that this could only be a guilty love; as yet he did not let her see his nets; as yet he only stood upon his honour.

"Hoo dus th' coo ya?"* she had asked of him one morning, soon after he had gone there.

And he answered, putting his arm about her, and toying with her golden hair, "Jasper Tudor, that is my name, Daisy, and you must always call me Jasper."

"It's a reet conny naam, I's capped wi' it. Jasper—Jasper—it's a bonny naam, it is, hawivver."

"I never liked it so well myself, Daisy, before to-day."

"I nivver heard tell er it afore; there's a deal er Toomas's an' Jooans an' a gude few er Abrahams, awe oop an' doon; bet there isn't a Jasper I'll promus yer. It's happen what they coo's a king or sick like girt fooak. Jasper, Jasper—a like it weel, varra."

And with many arch prettinesses did she shout his name upon the fells and scars, all that bright morning through.

* How do they call you?

Therefore from that day they were only Jasper and Daisy to each other. And hour by hour her unsuspected peril grew. But she, guileless, and pure, and trusting, ever walked in a delicious dream of happy, simple innocency. With his rod, only as a cunningly devised device to lead old Noah Hermon astray, Jasper Tudor went out to pass those bright early mornings in long ramblings with her. He did not think the time as yet had come when he might ask of her to love him as he would have her love. He did not think the time as yet had come when he might awake her from this dream, and talk nothing further to her about honour. And so each day she trusted him the more; and he saw how she trusted, and, because of what he meant to do, he was very glad.

. Sometimes from sunrise until the day was nearly getting to be noon, they would climb together the mountains of that beautiful valley, nor did they even tire in getting to " Helvellyn Man."* He had early per-

* A heap of stones on the summit of Helvellyn.

suaded her, when she would have spoken
of this to her father, that it might only
unnecessarily cause the old man to think
that evil would be coming to her. Jasper
Tudor also said in those days that he would
himself talk to her father concerning this
matter that was between them shortly.
And so guarded was he in the concealment
of his purpose, that she well believed that
which he urged was justified by the pureness
of his love ; therefore the fisher seemed to
fish ; and Noah Hermon saw nothing of
that which was hanging over his child.
And they met when the dew was heavy on
the grass, and did not part until the sun
was often high. Sometimes she would
" drink those perilous draughts of the vint-
age of love" by Griesdale Tarn, and sometimes they would wander over Kirkstone
into Troutbeck to the Mortal Man* by the
way of Hogarth's cottage ; and he would
lift her in his arms across the streams, and
chide her if her pretty feet got wet ; and so
did each of those bright sunny days bring

* An inn in Troutbeck.

her nearer to those clouds which as yet she could not see.

The old man, Daisy's father, meanwhile was fully persuaded that he had a lodger much and continuously given to the angle, and one who moreover must be following his craft with only clumsy flies—for it was not often that the fisher carried back a dish of fish; yet Noah Hermon knew of a long experience that the fervour of these fishers to cast their flies upon the water did not suffer if they did get nothing; therefore he took Jasper Tudor to be one of these, and as his Daisy was not forgetful of her cow, the danger she was hurrying on to was not at all suspected.

Jasper Tudor, both in his outward or his inner man, was not unpromisingly fashioned for a work so foul as this. Handsome in face, and striking in person, his voice, as has been said, came when he willed it with a strange and thrilling music on a woman's ear, and it had been very strange and thrilling when it floated in those soft murmurings about Daisy. But it was not the purpose of Jasper Tudor to toy in that valley with that girl for ever. He knew that none other than himself had got her heart. He knew how reverence had mingled with her love, and that such as he did might not, as she thought, have wrong in it—and the more unbounded her faith, the more unmeasured her trust, the more he compassed her about to destroy her.

"I must be leaving you soon, Daisy darling," he sadly said one morning, as they were standing near the stream of Griesdale under the shadows of Helvellyn; "should you care for me to go away?"

She was stunned by what he had told to her, and at the first she was speechless, and then she came near to him and twined her arm in his, and looking down upon her agony, he saw that her tears were falling on his breast.

"Waistomea!* waistomea! I's nae tea dra† bet wi' thee, Jasper," was all that she could cry.

This which he had spoken had come upon her as he meant it should. She could have

* Woe's me.   † Home.

no home without him, and when he heard that saying he knew that she was his.

"I only said those cruel words, Daisy, to see how much you loved me." And he caressed and comforted her as he bethought him, "she is mine, now she is mine;" and he pressed her closely to his heart as he thought of his possession. But he was very wrong indeed, and it was told to him for the first time in all the days that he had lived, that there could be a limit to the trust which he was minded to betray. She did not know how much, how terribly he meant to wrong her. She only knew that he would overshadow her with shame, and that the love he offered was a poisoned thing. She kneeled to him, she clung to his hand, and never had he seen a woman so bowed down.

"Jasper! Jasper! I's looved thee, me ain, wi' sick a loove, sooa girt, sooa trew. A isn't fit for thee, a knaa I's nowt bet a plaan sorry lass. Clod* ma a yon braaid-scar,† an' keel ma if ye be minded. Feyl‡ ma, Jasper, if

* Dash.　　† Broad stone.　　‡ Beat.

ye weel, an' I'll nit greet* a deal, bet dae
nit esk ma ta be dannet."† And then she
got up and said with a sad pleasing smile,
" Ye cud nit sarra thine lile Daisy thissen.‡
Ya cud nit, Jasper, ya's o'er ' trew.' "

Baffled as was his illicit love, he felt
within himself, as she pleaded against shame
at his knees, that she the rather had con-
quered, and how impossible it now was for
him to yield her up. Therefore he soothed
her and said he had a while ago but jested ;
and had she not told him, weeping on his
breast, that he was too true to ask of her
this shame ? And did she not believe in
that which she had said ? Then he kissed
her, and she was happy again.

If there must be, he bethought him as they
walked along, the mockery of a marriage just
to calm her, a marriage there shall be. I
can as easily presently be rid of her. I can
do with this girl as I will. And this was the
communing of his heart when he looked into

* Cry. † But do not ask me to be wicked.
‡ You could not serve your little Daisy like this.

the fathomless faith which was in her eyes, and asked of her plaintively to be his wife.

Now she knew that he had but jested with her a while ago, and the blush of love with which she answered him covered her beautiful face.

"I's maislikin* varra, a knaa, Jasper, bet a canna weel spak for joy; a hesn't ni porshon,† nit a fardun, bet I'll try tae knact.‡ I weel, hawivver, when ya taks ma ta Lunnon; an' a can meeak ya yer sarks,§ Jasper; an I'll hae nae maggets;‖ an' a wud leeve at pig-hall¶ wi ya if ye'll loove ma a deeal, Jasper. A cud nit bide wi'oot thy loove."

When he had had his answer from those lips, the devilry within him almost seemed to falter. Even he, as she told him of her changeless love, when she told to him how surely she was set upon abiding in his heart, even he was not so foul as was his wont to

---

* Foolish.   † Fortune.

‡ Knact is a Cumberland expression, which means to attempt to speak a less rude dialect.

§ Shirts.   ‖ Whims.   ¶ Hog-stye.

be, when he felt those burning kisses and heard those awful vows. The struggle was not long upon him, and he chose the better way. He would not do to her this great and this cowardly wrong. He would make her his wife before the world, and confess her before all men. He would prize her even as it was fit she should be prized. He would not be ashamed concerning her, even in the highest places. He did not care if the manner of her speech were rude. No one should despise this wild daisy that he meant to wear. He would set her beside him, and he would be loyal to the mighty love with which she so loved him.

But before the night of that day was gone he began to be otherwise minded about cleaving to her continually. He would marry her darkly, and not before the world; he would not confess before all men that he had had a cow-keeper's daughter to wife. Her little hands were badly browned, and would be to many an offence. And then she talked in such broad Westmoreland, and said such strange, plain things! Therefore he would

make of her his wife, and when it might be
well to cast her off she should be put away.

"Daisy, darling!" he fondly said to her,
when they met by the stream the next
morning, " I have something to say to you
—something that you must not tell to any
one so long as I live."

" I'll promus owt for ya, Jasper, I hae sick
a loove for ya; it's o'er girt for me lile
mouth ta spak."

" Can't you say ' such,' Daisy ? ' sick' is
such a nasty word !"

And she put up her little mouth to try.
"Sooch," she said ; " is't bettre, Jasper ?"

" Never mind, Daisy," he answered, coldly,
for he was well persuaded that she who could
only speak of such things as "sick" and "girt"
would not do to sit in black velvet at his
table.   "And now let me tell you what I
had to say ;" and he leant over her, and whispered in her ear.

She paled at what he said, but quickly
answered—

" I loove ye joost as weel, a dae, hawivver."

During the early part of the following

week he was away in London, making some preparations for their marriage; and immediately after his return they were married, without the knowledge of Noah Hermon, at the little chapel of Jesus, at Troutbeck. He had persuaded her that, as yet, it were better not to tell her father. She had struggled against this harsh resolve of his with smiles and with tears; but when he had been angered, and had said, "Daisy, you do not trust me, or you would believe I did this for the best," then she had answered him no more, for verily and indeed she did trust him altogether. Jasper Tudor had, it is true, once intended not to delay acknowledging her honestly, and as beseemed him; but letters which had reached him when he was in London had afterwards altered his purpose, and now he was minded he would for some time put it off. When she would have bleached those little hands, when the manner of her speech should be less rude, then it might be that he would acknowledge her.

Not having concluded, when he first came

to the little inn at Ullswater, to remain there more than a few days, he had desired his letters to be sent to London, and one of these, from his father, had been urgent in wishing for him to come home at once; whilst another from his mother was full of a new beauty that she had chosen for him, and had set her heart upon his marrying. But his passion for the daughter of Noah Hermon the rather grew by reason of his absence from her, and he had confided to her that which would now make it the less easy for him to cast her off. He had sometimes thought, when he was in London, that as this girl asked marriage for her love, that he would not have it at the price; but when he saw what others were who were accounted beautiful, and he thought how meanly they would rank by Daisy's side, therefore he would marry her, not because he meant to put her by their side, but because he purposed that this peerless girl should be his own.

Three weeks after they were married, Jasper Tudor left her hurriedly, upon the lying plea that he had been summoned home.

But when she clung to him, and said that they should never part, he comforted her by the assurance that he would shortly return to claim and to acknowledge her.

"Then," he had said, "I will take my Daisy with me, and tell to all you are my very own." And with this lie he left her.

Months went by, and Jasper Tudor never came back. Presently she thought the number of his letters had fallen off; and then it came to be that she only got a little cold one now and then. And now it would be soon, she knew, no longer possible for her to keep back from her father that she would early be a mother. She wrote to Jasper, too, in words that would have melted stones, for her heart was very near to breaking; but at long intervals he only returned to her icy answers, bidding her remember what she had been when he had found her with that cow, and what he was; and once he had told her she had better give up writing if she could not spell; but then he sent to her a cheque upon his bankers, that so she might get baby-linen, and have a decent woman with her when she should be lying-in. She had undertaken to Jasper Tudor, that she would in nowise tell of their marriage, until such time as he might consent, to any one, not even to her father; and now that there were in that place hard sayings concerning her shame, he exacted the inexorable fulfilment of that which she had promised to the very letter. "It would ruin my prospects, Daisy," he wrote. "Do not ask this thing of me. I have already yielded much, for are you not my wife? It would greatly anger my father to do this which you wish. It would grieve my mother, who, I must tell you, has very correct tastes, Edith, and she would be shocked to hear you talk of ' girt ' and ' sick ;' and there are, also, many other difficulties about it ; but if they can at any time be overcome, I will let you know. I am glad to hear, from what you say, that your hands are a better colour, and that you do not talk so broadly. It is spelt talk, not *tauk*, as you have written it. Much offence would be given to many people if you spoke like this in London. I am

going away from here for a little; you had
better not write, perhaps, as your letters
might be opened. I sometimes almost think
that you did not do quite well in asking me
to marry you. When you are recovered you
might go out as a wet-nurse, and it would
be best if you said that you were single;
this is thought nothing of amongst ladies;
and then you would be able to get your own
living, which I know you would prefer. My
only wish is to see you happy."

And after that she had done reading this,
she went out and hid herself; and so, un-
timely, did the drooping and the blighted
Daisy pass into a mother, whilst the finger
of shame was pointed at her, and the finger
was that of the most respectable people.

Noah Hermon had got to hear of that
terrible thing which it was said was coming
on his child, through a friendly and a stately
maiden lady, who distributed coals at Christmas, and scandal throughout all the seasons.

"I am very grieved for you, Mr. Hermon, very; but I always thought your
daughter was a little bold. When she is

well again an effort must be made to get her where she may be brought to see how dreadful has been her sin. I hope God will forgive her, but we must be strict, and as a Christian woman, knowing what my obligations are, I shall take care she is not for the future noticed here. An example, Mr. Hermon, must be made."

And then she went out, charged with her Christian obligations, to order the casting of the stones.

Then there entered in the second Christian, who had also obligations like unto the first.

" Lord, barn, Noah, what is coom amang th' lasses er this spot? I's thinkin' th' dule* hes evven thrawn his cloob owar 'em, they er oa gaan craisy, they er shamful, they er, hawevver—nin on 'em wed, bet they hev their happron oop,† modesty is clean geean oot o' t' coontry."

" Ay, ay, Betty, that's trew enoo, that ·

---

* Devil.

† A Westmoreland saying, signifying that a woman seems likely to become a mother.

geean'd when ya wor a lass; bet isn't there a deal er oogly steeans thrawn by Chreestan fooak?"

Then after that Betty had gone out, this third Christian entered in, and the obligations of this third one were not like to those of the first and second, but seemed to be a little loose.

"It's awe spite, Noah—tak oop, tak oop; it's awe spite, nowt i' th' ward else. Daisy's graaid* lass, I'll warr'n es; bet oor nebbus,† Noah, is sick a spiteful gang; if they cud they'd evven poo ‡ thy Daisy ea bits; they be ready te steean her!"

Then this lax Christian woman, who would not cast her stone, went out; and the old man, before that this great sorrow killed him, took Daisy to his heart, and said that *he* did not accuse her.

But Edith, after she was safe, did write this, even though her letter should be opened:—

"DEAREST HOOSBAND,

"Thy lile Daisy is saaf an' weel; oor

* Honest or virtuous.   † Neighbour.   ‡ Pull.

barn is a tinny lass, an' sooa varra like tama. Hoo shud I coo her?"

But she did not say to him that one con-
demning sermon had been preached about
her in the parish church, and that she was
otherwise numbered amongst the fallen. It
is not likely that he would have cared, even
if she had so told him. But he was angered
because of this letter; angered that he had
taken to be his wife one who could only
after this sort write and spell. And he said,
"I am so glad that your baby is like you,
Daisy! I know so little of girls' names—
but will you call it Sybil?" After this
there was more; and then when she had read
that which he had further written, she fell
upon the earth, as though her young life
had followed her blasted confiding.

He would leave her, he said, from that
day for ever—alone! She, once his darling,
his Daisy, his pretty pet! He would leave
her alone—with her changeless love and her
little one!

CHAPTER VII.

WITH THE PAST.

MINNA Norman could not have got free of
the strangely clinging woman, however
much she might have willed it. She had,
indeed, heard how these sort of hysterical
scenes sometimes ended in the stripping of
houses, or at least of their halls. But
Minna did not think this woman's hands
were given to picking or to stealing. She
had, it is true, been told that those who did
these things were generally well instructed
performers, and were usually emotionally
seized, as was this woman, before they
seized upon the silver. Minna had seen
certain of them in the picture papers, and
she remembered that they had looked to be
benevolent and tearful. And then, too, had
she not also been told of begging impostors·

journeying about with all the apparatus of grief and larceny, and of melting tears that were much given to come very freely before the melting down of the spoons. Here were the tears; and Minna did not know but what it might be as well that the woman and the spoons should not be got together. She bethought her it was hard to understand what could be the purpose. of this woman coming these two times, and why that which there might be to say could not as well be said under the beeches. Perhaps it would be for the best if the bell were to be rung, and some one else got upon the spot; for if this woman had not it on her mind to steal, it yet might be concluded that she would presently faint. But Minna Norman, the while she thought that she was only doing weakly, did, nevertheless, shrink from setting a hireling to inquire of this woman roughly what she meant. If Minna did know anything of the outward seeming of a sorrow that was neither feigned nor fictitious, then she persuaded herself, with her hand almost on the bell rope, that there was at least no imposition in this agony, no counterfeit about these tears. She knew that her aunt, when she came to hear of it, would say that it was not wise to let this woman lie upon the floor. And Minna also thought it was not wise; but she would the rather that the woman should presently turn round and steal, than that she should be suspected if she were no thief. Therefore, as yet, she resolved she would not ring. The woman, moreover, whatever might be her purpose, did not look to be ill-fed. She could scarcely be starving, and was ashamed to beg. She could not have come there after broken victuals. But Minna had heard that those who seemed to be respectable were often pinched, and had some time fasted— therefore she would ask the woman if she wanted food.

" Tell me what can I do for you ; is it that you are hungry ? " But the woman only very sadly shook her head, and still was speechless.

Then Minna bethought her, was this bowed down one before her, stooping under

the weight of such a burden of crushing
sorrow that she could no longer stand up
and bear it alone? The more that Minna Norman in her gentleness would have soothed,
so much the more a great deal was the
stricken creature bound with terrible pa-
roxysms that almost seemed to tear her.
Minna at the last felt for her purse, that so
she might offer alms, but when the woman
saw this movement she looked up and cried
out——

"Nae, nae, bonny an' loovin' Miss, bet I'll
hev non er it. I hasn't coom'd for brass. I
isn't coom'd ta esk ya ta fend* me. I hasn't
meand† er bein' hoongered. I isn't tur-
moild‡ for vittals; bet I's tummelt§ inta
a deal er trooble; an' soomteems I's welly‖
fit ta dee er greetin.¶ Ye glenders** er ma,
as weel ye may; bet I's graaid,†† a is
indeed."

"Then, my, poor woman," said Minna,
taking in her own the little hand that was

---

* Help or provide for.   † Complained.
‡ Troubled.   § Fallen.   ‖ Almost.
¶ Crying.   ** Stares.   †† Honest.

put out to her. "Tell me what your trouble is, and I will help you if I can—tell to me what is your sorrow : are you ill, or unhappy?" And then she further inquired very softly, "have you lost any one you love?"

Now the asking of this was a great deal more than that overweighted woman could bear. If Minna had said rough things, it might be that that woman would have turned upon her, and have spoken all that there was to speak. She who in her wretchedness was bowed down there, had come into that room believing she could tell her story—the dark and terrible story of her life—calmly, and without being so overset, without this speechless agony, without those choking tears. She had not meant to break down so utterly as she had broken down. She had meant to struggle and be strong, at least until her story should be ended. And now, before she had made of it a beginning, those words, so softly and so sweetly spoken, asked of her if she had lost any one she loved.

It has been said that it was more than she could bear, those gentle words upon those lips. She got up from her knees, and crouched and looked as if she would have sprung on Minna, and with a cry that rang through the house, she fell forward on her face.

"Sybil, Sybil, a hesni coom for vittuls, ní for brass. I's yer ain puir mudther. I's yer ain puir mudther."

When those who had been startled by that cry came crowding in, she who had so cried was lying senseless on the floor. Wau-chope, who in such situations was not given to deliver a measured judgment upon appearances, now declared that her young mistress was being badly taken in, and that when the horse patrol went by he had better be stopped. She further pronounced decisively for an attempt at extortion or felony, and went over Minna's dressing-case to see that none of the silver tops had been purloined. She would then have proceeded to extend her search to the woman, had she not been otherwise ordered. Therefore she took

herself out in the fulness of her conviction,
to tell it about below stairs that there was
"a hartful himposter a going through er
tricks in Miss Minna's room."

"What's her game?" loftily asked the
butler, Rooke; "them dodgers never is
two of 'em alike."

"Why, she's a kicking and a screaming
fearful, Rooke—hall of a eap on the floor.
Ho, my! hit's hawful!"

"They is a hartful lot, and they're
halways a falling about when they don't
want to be collared! I suppose she's a
finish sort of a female——"

"That ain't nothing to you, Rooke.
She's a orrid nasty thing!" said Wauchope,
as she bounced out of the lower room.

Now Wauchope and Rooke looked with
favour on each other; and the handmaid
was angered because that the butler now
seemed to be concerned about divers orders
of fine women.

"What does all this mean, Minna?"
inquired Lady D'Aeth, who had come upon
the spot immediately.

"I don't know indeed, aunt, what it means; but I think, poor thing, that she can't be quite right. Help me, Wauchope, to lift her up on to my bed," said Minna Norman, as the maid came in flushed with Rooke's inconstancy.

" Put *her* on *your* bed, miss? I 'opes I's a respectable female ; and Rooke and me's kept company, and he's very purticlar, miss, what I touches. I ain't a given to answerin' no one ; and I's willin' to make myself generally useful, but I wasn't engaged to do this sort of work," answered the maid, who thought that if some one was not quite right, that some one could be none other than her young mistress.

"Do as you are desired, Wauchope," said Lady D'Aeth, with firmness.

" Yes, my lady; and I'd like to be leaving this day month."

" You shall leave earlier, Wauchope, if I can get suited ; and now lift that poor woman on to Miss Norman's bed," answered Lady D'Aeth, who saw that if there had been any other attempt to impose, the woman's unconsciousness was, at least, not pretended.

"Oh please, my lady," implored Wauchope, when her work was done, " I'm very sorry for what I said just now, and I don't want to leave. I's so 'appy, and you, my lady, and Miss Norman's so kind! and I likes the place, and the vittals is abundant. This woman's come after the sittiation, I know she has; it's her who came before. And please let me stop, for Rooke says he can't marry me yet, as he can't get a shop nowhere to soot him; and he'll be spiteful hawful, and wont wait." And Wauchope got upon her knees, and entreated that her own decision might not be recorded against her.

"I will speak to you about this, Wauchope, at some other time; but I must tell you that you have ill chosen this day to worry and annoy Miss Norman."

"Never mind about me, aunt," pleaded Minna. " Wauchope's quite right; this poor woman is the same who came about the place once before. She met me outside just now, under the beeches, and said she had something very particular to say to me; and although I was in such trouble myself, I did not like to say I would not hear her. You are not angry with me, aunt?"

"No, my love; I am very far from that. But I am sorry that at the time of your great trial this annoyance should also have come upon you. I only think it was not wise to bring this woman up here, Minna. Tell me, now, what was it she wanted so very particularly to tell you—so very particularly, that it could not be said under the beeches?"

"She said nothing, aunt, and did nothing but cry, poor thing! and kept on kissing my hands. And when, just before she fell down there where you saw her, I thought she was going to be ill, she looked so wild; and after that she called me Sybil, and said she was my mother."

"It's very odd," said Lady D'Aeth. "Had she not been here before, I should have said she had escaped from confinement somewhere; but these things are so well acted now, that I am almost afraid it looks a little suspicious, Minna."

"If you mean, aunt, that you think she came here meaning to do wrong, I think you are mistaken. She would not let me even offer her money: all is very strange; but I am sure that it will be explained."

By this time Wauchope's hydropathic efforts and applications to restore animation were beginning to tell, for, as has been seen, she had been persuaded to throw water into the face of the woman, very freely administering the element, although she knew the so-called intruder had got in there to carry away her situation. .

"She's a coming to, my lady; she's a gasping, and her 'ips his quivering," said Wauchope, as the woman began slowly and with effort to sit up on the bed.

"Whaar's ma lile conny Sybil? Haista* takken she away frae me agin? Whaar is't yee, Sybil, ma puir bairn?"

"I'm afraid it's in her head, Minna," said Lady D'Aeth.

"Nae, nae, ma lady, ye's for ivver wrong; it's nit at neb. I's taukin trew I'll ensure

* Have you.

ye; bet it's in ma heart that I's freated* a goode few years. It's bin bet a dreet† teem wimma, it has, hawivver. I's coom'd ta telt it ye awe." And as she so spoke, she looked round upon them all.

"To tell us what, my good woman?" asked Lady D'Aeth. "We none of us think ill of you; we only ask you to explain your coming here."

"I's evven here, ma lady, ta telt ya that I's yon's ain trew mudther."

"When you talk like this it is that you will not let us think well of you. You do not seem to be destitute. Have you no friends who will take care of you?"

"Friends, ma lady! it's a while sen ivver a waar rank wi' sick like. Ye's a gae kind deaam,‡ an' has mappen a deal er friends. I's evven alecan at world—evven alecan!" And as she sadly spoke, some shadows of the past called back showed in her deep and earnest eyes. "If ya bethink yerssels I's tryin' ta stoof ya wi' lees, there's he at hoose who cud tell ya varra sendry."§

---

* Mourned. † Long, tedious. ‡ Lady. § Different.

"You came in here," said Lady D'Aeth, "because you had something very particular to say, that——"

"An' hesn't a telt it ta ya, an' isn't it serious particlar, varra?" And she looked round, and then she whispered, "If Meester Massareene, when he discerns ma, ses ta ye she lees, a don't knaa th' ooman at awe, I'll meeak he tell trew afoore a far oer girt coompany er this—a weel that; I isn't dannet*, a isn't, hawivver."

Now, Lady D'Aeth, in her heart of hearts, believed this woman to be very mad; but this open reference to Massareene at once determined her that there should be no condemnation, no arraignment even of this story as a fantastic fiction, when proof was offered to her that minute in her own drawing-room. She believed this woman to be only strange and weakly and disordered; but if Mr. Massareene would only say that he had never seen the woman, then would there be an end to doubt. Therefore she went down

* A wicked woman.

to tell the minister of those things that had
been going on upstairs.

And Fabian Massareene heard all that
was told to him from end to end, and did
not even smile. Once he had been shot at
in the lobby of the House of Commons, and
he knew that men who moved where he
was moving, were often much importuned
by mere harmless lunatics. And he also
felt when he had been spoken to concerning
this woman, that neither she nor any other
woman could tell to him, or of him, anything that he did not care to hear. That
which he had done he had done perfectly;
he had destroyed reputations ; but then, had
he not also destroyed the witness that it was
his act ? He had always been at some pains
to arrange for the suppression of those who
might be likely to be vexatious and appear
against him. There was only one he could
not answer to, and she, he knew, was dead.
He would not have to answer to her *here*.
Therefore he concluded that the woman must
be mad who had said that he could testify
about her; and then he could not, without

some suspicion, well refuse to help to put
an end to the reliability of a story that had
the seeming of being so wild.

"I have seen many of these unhappy
cases, in my time, Lady D'Aeth. There is
indeed occasionally, a strange method in
their madness; so much so that it is most
difficult very often to upset, at first, the pro-
bability of what they may say; but get
them on to any other subject, and you per-
ceive their infirmity at once. I shall be
curious to hear what this poor creature has
to say about me."

Now Fabian Massareene had said this
because he did not know who might be this
woman, and what might be her story. Therefore he concluded that it would be best to
shake her testimony before she spoke. So
Lady D'Aeth went back, that she might
lead the stranger down to Mr. Massareene.

"Sybil, ma ain, coom wimma tull* him.
He has nivver set eyes er yer es what ya are."

And then they all went down the stairs,
Wauchope bringing up the rear; Rooke,

* To.

the while, holding himself as a contingent,
to appear if the woman should proceed to
violence.

Massareene, in that minute after Lady
D'Aeth had left him, went back to a bright
autumn time which had some eighteen
years gone by. Sybil!—that name!—but
yet it could not be. Yet, if it could—if
Sybil, and if Sybil's mother lived? And as
this fearful thought sat on him, he heard
that they were coming.

The woman whom they were leading in,
when she saw before her the tall, command-
ing, stately presence, did not wait for any
leave to speak. She got free of them all,
and running up to where the minister stood,
she looked him full, and without shrinking,
in the face; and then she crept up nearer,
and whispered, "Jasper, it's thine ain lile
Daisy." He started as though he were
wounded to the death, and she went on,
"Fabian, ya meeak'd ma promus a while ago
that I'd for ivver hod ma din aboot oor
bein' wed, till ye telt for ma a meet spak er
it. An' I moost, Fabian, be spakin' noo, if

ye weel or nit, for it's evven yar ain sweet
barn ye are sooa keen ta be weddin'. Ye'll
nit slat* ma frae ye noo, darlin'; ye'll nit
say to these fooak that I's widdersful† ta
cheeat 'em. Ye'll nit say ya nivver knaa'd
ma, Fabian?" And she kneeled to his feet
and kissed them.

He could not say he did not know her.
He could not tell them to take her away
and put her out. But then, he would not
have said it even if he could, for the voice,
the look, and the past rushed back like a
torrent upon Massareene.

"O God! it's my wife! it's Daisy, my
dead Daisy," he cried, and staggering back,
he leaned heavily against the wall, gasping
and fighting for breath, with his hand
strained hard on his left side.

"I's keelt he! I's keelt he! Dunnet* dee,
Fabian! dunnet dee!"

"Yes, Edith, it will kill me; this day, I
feel, will be my last; but I thank God that
He has let me speak before I die."

They led him gently to a couch; a heavy

* Throw.　　† Trying.　　‡ Do not.

sweat—the sweat of agony—had broken out
upon him, as the spasms at his heart came
quicker and quicker. It would be hours before
a doctor could be fetched; and if one could
be got at once, there was no medicine that
might reach this pain. He knew that so
long as he lived, in his body he should never
be again at ease; but he thought that in his
mind he might have peace.

The woman who so lately was accounted
to be very mad was yet kneeling at his side,
wiping his brow as the heavy drops ran
down, and murmuring the while—" He's
trew t' his loove—he ains* ma, he ains ma."

He did not push her roughly from him;
he did not push her from him at all. That
which was on him was death; it was getting
to be very near; and in his anguish he
asked that it might be soon; but before he
should be dying, he would clear this woman.
It was not because he knew that she could
show the marriage lines; it was not because
of what he knew that she could prove—but
that terrible wrong of eighteen years should
be told to them all. He did not dare

* Owns.

inquire of himself if it could be wiped off from his soul. If he had fallen where mercy might not take him up, yet would he be his own accuser of this scarlet sin for Daisy's sake. He would be the true husband of this wife at last.

To look upon her who knelt there to him, as in his agony he sought to answer smile for smile, the woman who had come to be a serving maid, her caresses not forbidden by the favourite Minister of England, was that which no one there could read. Then she bent over him, and they heard her saying, "Fabian, I's keelt thee wimma tauk, I's keelt thee. Ye's bawn* frae mae. Munea† gie thee oop? Munca be left aleean, thine lile puir Daisy?"

"I shall have left you by to-morrow, Daisy."

"Nae, nae, nit to-morn,‡ Fabian, nit to-morn. I canna bide wi'oot thee." Then she covered her face in his breast, and when next she looked into his eyes she asked, "Oh, isn't oor Sybil a conny yan an' a

* Going.   † Must I.   ‡ To-morrow.

sweet? It's evven oor ain bairn, Fabian,
that ya wud hae wed." And as he shuddered
and groaned at this which was said, Edith
turning to their child motioned her to come
near to the side of the dying man, saying
passionately, " You may loove he weel, Sybil,
for he's thine ain fadther." And the stricken
statesman, with a murmur of love, held out
his arms, and took his child into his bosom.
He gazed into her eyes, he covered her
with kisses. "Too late, too late!" he
sobbed. "O God, thou hast been merciful
to let me see her now! Closer, come closer,
darling, do not leave me whilst I live—
whilst—whilst—these pains of hell have
gotten hold upon me." And in his growing
agony he entreated he might die.

Rooke had been disquieted at his meals
to go for as many doctors as he could find;
and as the sufferings of Massareene became
the more intense, plasters and poultices and
fomentations were ordered before the coming
of even the first of the leeches. The
tenderest touch was torment, and presently
the minister motioned for all to leave the

room but Lady D'Aeth, his wife and child. Then, when only such remained as he desired, raising himself up to speak, he said slowly and emphatically to Lady D'Aeth: "She whom you thought so mad, she *is* my lawful wife, my wife that I have long thought dead. Edith, tell them all; cover nothing of my shame and sin; whilst I have got the life left to say that it is true." And then he sank back into his Daisy's arms, whilst he fought for the breath to come. Then they gathered round and listened to the story of that love, and that desertion, from the lips of Massareene's wife, that has been already given in this history.

Now of her own will or inclination, let it be recorded, Edith Massareene would have said but little that would have showed that her husband had not been loyal to his love. To her, that which was gone by was blotted out. Her husband had confessed her, and she who was raised even at the last to be his wife, would not sink to be his judge. Had she not been, when he took

her from that cow, rude in her speech and
wild in her ways? Could he have set her
by his side and not have been ashamed?
So did Edith Massareene inquire of herself
if her husband's sin had not been justified
because that she had been of low degree.
With him the struggle was past. As he
had been, so was he not now. Not even
for a moment had it come into his mind that
he would discredit or deny her. Nor was
he so purposed because that it would have
been vain to have disowned her. Fabian Massareene knew that that which had stricken
him was death. The physicians, when they
came together round about him might of one
accord conspire to tell him to hope, and with
their medicines,so long as he lived,they might
get for him a little ease in that aching and
that tortured side. But it was not the consci-
ousness that he so soon must die, or that
the woman who had so strangely spoken
could trace the things which she had
spoken back; but it was this, that Fabian
Massareene's whole life had come before
him, and he repented himself of all the ill

that he had done. And when he should be dead, the story of his life would be told in an octavo—and men would say that it was bright, and true, and clean, whilst that of it which had been true, and clean, and bright, would not be told at all. And his wife that he had cast off those many years, with her wife-like, holy love, would the rather have held her peace, lest her tongue should slip, and tell of something that might not do him honour, had he not been there himself to bear the stain that could never be wiped out.

The history of those eighteen years of the life of Edith Massareene as told by herself ·was a long one, and put into a few words it recorded this.

Some time after the birth of her child, she had, as has been already said, got a letter from Fabian Massareene, in the which, after asking whether it would not be well to call the little one Sybil, he went on to say, that from many causes he could never own her to the world as his wife. He had also said that he might have lied, and have led her to believe that some day he would confess her; but he would not so lie, for he never did mean to confess her. He thought that she would sorrow, but it would not be for ever. He had greatly sacrificed himself in marrying her at all; and he had done so much for her virtue, that she must do this for his dignity. And then he went on to say that he meant to do everything that was honourable, and to this end he had set aside a sum sufficient for the decent maintenance of herself and child, the interest of which would be paid to her so long as she lived, at a place he went on to indicate; and that in the event of her dying before the death or marriage of her daughter, that sum would be doubled, and would be possessed by her child. Edith had at the first reading of this resolved that from one who set her so low, and who could do by her as this man meant to do, she would at least take nothing. She could see that she had no longer any place in Massareene's heart. The money would be paid, and he had so ordered it, that he need

not fear what might befall her or her child.
The stories of their lives need never come
before him—they would be for ever kept
out of the sight of his eyes—therefore at the
first she purposed that for herself she would
not touch it; and she was also resolved,
when the occasion offered, to let it appear
to him and to all who knew her that she
was dead, so that the benefit which from the
moment of her dying should belong to her
little one, might at once accrue. And, other
than this, because of the things which were
said against her, she felt that she must
hide. It was told of her that her love had
been guilty, and that in shame had she
become a mother. And she must not answer
at all to these things. She had sworn to
him to hold her peace till he should let her
speak, therefore she would hide and be as
one that was dead.

So minded, Edith alone told what she
meant to do to the woman who had nursed
her through her lying-in; who had spoken
comfortable words, when leading Christian
women had gathered up their gowns about

them as they passed her door; to the only woman who had not seemed to sniff contagion when she, the outcast, went abroad. To her the wife of Fabian Massareene told her history. To her did Edith tell of that resolve to be counted no more among the living; and to her she left in sacred trust the care of the little Sybil. Now, Fabian Massareene, in the settling of that money upon Edith and her child, had still been Jasper Tudor, so that his name and the girl's might not, in this matter, inconveniently come together.

A few days later, it was told through the valley that Edith Hermon, who had been wronged by Jasper Tudor, had been drowned by her own hand in the lake of Ullswater; so that those who were persuaded of her sin before, now went about gathering others to their creed, and saying that she had gone into the water because she had been there driven by her guilt. And after this they bore themselves so much the higher to show they could not fall. It never got across the mountain into Troutbeck, where Massa-

reene was married, this story of Edith's
fall and end, or it might have been that
the true history of her love would have been
told.

Many of those things that Edith had been
known to wear, were found on the steep
rocky side where the bluish water of the
lake is in depth a hundred yards. The body
was dragged for through many weeks. It
was never found; until at the last, the search
was given over, and those who had been
seeking for the corpse, were persuaded that
it had got under some big rock or stone.
But although in the end gunpowder was
exploded under the water, the body of Edith
was never recovered. So it came to be concluded amongst certain of the more chari-
tably superstitious, that the exceeding load
of her guilt kept her body from rising, as it
inevitably would interfere with the buoyancy
of her soul. And so she was no more named
amongst them—she, who had never thought
that care could come upon her, till the morning of that day when she met that fisher by
the stream, and sung once too often that
song to her cow.

And after that, when the drags were hung up, a very terrible sermon was preached, and Edith's doom was divided into three heads for the space of fifty minutes.

With the sure knowledge that her child was in faithful keeping, she who was accounted to be dead went out into the world to get her bread. After three years were ended she came disguised by night to see if her little one was well, and found that the woman to whom it had been left had lately died, and that the child was in the hands of one Gideon Cuyp, an undertaker living at Black Moss, in Cumberland, of whom excellent things were spoken.

Edith remembered to have once heard of this man as in some way, if distantly, connected with herself; and from that night when she learnt where her little daughter was, through all the years that Sybil was growing up, and was known to Black Moss as Minna Norman, by which name the mother had desired her little one should be known, Edith found many ways of seeing her child unobserved and unsuspected.

Now, Gideon Cuyp had not at any time known that she whom it was said in Black Moss he had benevolently adopted, and to whose benefit he had so beneficently devoted a fourth of that which was all her own, was in any way a blood relation. The only connexion that the undertaker looked to was the possession which was reserved to Sybil, and until that should be lost or diverted, he did not feel to be necessitated to make any further inquiries. Sybil had come into the undertaker's hands as Minna Norman, with whose bringing up one Jasper Tudor seemed to have charged himself. This was enough knowledge for Gideon Cuyp to have in this matter, and he did not propose to himself to ask any questions, so long as payment of that which was allowed was so regularly made; and he had therefore never heard the true story of the birth of Minna Norman.

Never before now, but once, had Edith Massareene yielded to the temptation of trusting herself in the presence of her child, and that once, as has been told, she had come offering to be her maid.

" An' noo," she murmured softly in her husband's ear, when that which she had to say was ended, " I shud hae kipt ma promus, Fabian, if a hed nit sen this at paper a bit sen, nivver ta tell ta owt that a wur wed t'ye." And then she showed to him the lines in the county paper, in the which it was set forth, on the best authority, that he was going to marry Minna Norman.

He heard it all, all on to the end; and then the worst pain at his heart was because of his great sin. He did not think what his father or his mother might say, or what would come to their grey hairs when it was told to them what he had been; nor did he think what England might say. He only thought of that which he had brought upon this woman; and after he had seemed, from the manner of his words, to have been in the shadowy past, he drew Sybil to his knee, and the big tears fell upon her upturned face.

" My pretty one, you will not curse me? Speak, speak!—the time is short. Oh, think of me, not bitterly, when I am gone!—be

gentle, sweet one, to your father's memory.
Oh, Sybil, if there may be mercy for a
wretch like I, we yet may meet again !"

· "Father, dear father, there may be mercy
for us all! You must not die—you——"

And he put his hands before his eyes, as
if to drag aside some veil that was before
them.

"It is I, your little Sybil, father—don't
you know me ?"

Yes, it was his own one who was kneeling
at his knees as the films of death were
settling on him ; his very own, who, of all
the women he had ever seen, he had only
loved in the face of the world.

"Yes, yes; I know you now. Sybil,
come closer, for I cannot see ; it's growing
dark. Edith, our darling *is* like you—as
like you as you said. When all is over,
teach her to sing that song that you used to
sing to your cow." Then he covered his
face with his hands, and cried—"No, no,
Edith, I cannot own you—what will my
father say? The cowkeeper's daughter !
you are not my wife !" And then, as though

awaking from some fearful dream, he went on—"What are they saying? that I shall not own you, Daisy—my pretty pet—my own! They shall not take you from me! Edith, the trout are rising in the stream. Sing, darling and pretty pet — sing that song to your cow!"

These were nearly the last words of Fabian Massareene. He had early asked for the vicar, but when Guy Melchior came he did not know him.

As the night went on his agonies were terrible to see, and in quick succession spasm followed spasm. At midnight he had seemed to be for a moment a little easier; and there was a smile on his face—the smile on which he had ever staked so much—and a movement on his lips.

Edith bent over, if it might be, to catch and register the precious whispering of dissolution; and she was always persuaded that he said, "Sing that song, Daisy—sing to your cow!" For even in the awful mists *the* love of his life stood clear. And then whilst Sybil knelt to kiss him there was a

sigh and a shudder—England's favourite
had passed away; and the doctor, seeing
that his hour had come, feeling for the pulse
that was for ever still, had told to those
assembled there that Fabian Massareene
was dead !

CHAPTER VIII.

THE NEW DEAN.

THE intelligence of the death of Fabian
Massareene, which was communicated in a
second edition of the *Times* to the country,
was received with wide-spread gloom. The
people felt much as they did some time later
feel, when that bay horse shied on Consti-
tution Hill, and England was sorrowing for
Sir Robert Peel. It depressed all men, and
it depressed the funds. It was even asked
how his great virtues should be commemo-
rated, before it was discovered that his virtues
had only lived between one noon and one
night at Black Moss Abbey. The ministerial papers were persuaded that he would
be carried into Westminster Abbey, whilst
the more fervid and descriptive of these
prints called on the City to contend for the

"revered dust," and put it in S. Paul's. It was in the first moments of the nation's mourning reasoned that there was no one with the capacity to supply his place, although it might easily be seen, by looking upon certain groups, that there were not wanting those who could, with abundant fitness, take his salary. But after this, an evening paper, that did the bidding of the Government, wrote that the funeral would be quietly and privately ordered, and that there were circumstances which made it inexpedient that his burying should be in Westminster Abbey. Then, whilst it was being asked what this could mean, it got to be told how he had died. The print that had so demanded of the City to have the "revered dust" in S. Paul's, now wrote of the dead in a manner that was not so reverent. One paper that the Cabinet commanded did make a decent show of sheltering the now bespattered dead; but in four-and-twenty hours its proprietary begged of its employers that this decent show over the body might be abandoned. And so Fabian Massareene

was carried into a Yorkshire churchyard.
Guy Melchior read the office; and the
father and the mother of the dead were
there; and besides these there were none.
After the grave had been .filled in, Guy
Melchior went up to the childless two, and
would have spoken comfortable words, but
they would not hear him. They cried out,
" We are ashamed; we are ashamed; we
will go and hide ourselves ;" and stooping
with their load, they went, and were, until
their own death, hidden. Then, when they
were a little later gathered to their rest, it
was told that to Sybil were willed the
Massareene gems.

The early publication of the minister's
biography, from authentic sources, was
threatened by more than one publisher of
repute. Whilst the expectant country
waited for the appearance of the announced
octavos, some scenes from his life and his
amours, with coloured prints, for a. penny,
were offered through all the ducts and chan-
nels of the pest streets of the Strand ; and
a large issue of " the song to the cow" was

got rid of in the same direction. How the confessions of the minister got about was on this wise.

Rooke, the butler, who subscribed to certain cheap and warmly written prints, after possessing himself, by divers means, of Wauchope's confidence—she having been an outside listener, after she had been put out of the room, when the story of Massareene's life was told—supplied the matter for "the scenes," with many saleable and pungent additions of his own. But "the song to the cow"—an appropriated masterpiece of some forgotten libertine in the pastoral line —was wholly borrowed from a ballad that had been seized before it could be sung.

This was what befel the memory of the once high favourite—hoarse brawlers shouted the sum of his vices in the streets of London, and, mixed up with the profligacies of notorious voluptuaries, the saving scene of his life—the last—was scarcely ever spoken of but to be derided. The journals which had once exhibited their servility, and tasted his patronage, now covered his memory with vituperation, according to the text of their later instructions; and such of the godly as had consorted with him caused their studied staying away from his funeral to be conspicuously paraded. Once had Fabian Massareene been very like to an idol; but now, the people repented themselves that they had ever worshipped him at all.

In other and in higher spheres, such managerial mothers as had not been able to effect an alliance with the minister, now solemnly and triumphantly received the congratulations of their friends upon his having been declined in time. They had been tempted to take him, they said, but Providence had mercifully directed them otherwise. He had seemed to be all that woman could desire, but they, thank God, had got to see beneath the surface. And there were many mothers who could have had him, but who wouldn't, and who after this sort acknowledged the interference of Providence.

Nor were the sycophants who had been the minister's *quondam* followers any the less slow to disavow the policy that they themselves had once chiefly applauded. It was intolerable, they said, in clusters and in chorus, that their very reserved intercourse with him should now be overstated into a familiarity. They had always thought that it would come to this; they had always been persuaded that he was not that which he appeared to be; only they had held their peace because he had been so greatly sought that they durst not speak; and like the managerial mothers, they also thanked God that they had not fallen down before the minister. Others there were who said that he had more offended in his dying than in his living, and they looked upon those words, which in his last agonies had declared his wife to have been some time a cowkeeper's daughter, to be the crowning infamy of a shameful life. They pronounced it to have been " so deuced unnecessary." They, too, had looked upon cowkeepers' daughters; but then they had not married them. Had the cowkeeper's wench been Massareene's mistress, and his child the child of sin, then he would have been infinitely lifted up in their nice regards. They did not care whether he might have done to her a wrong; but now they pronounced him to have been not right in the head.

"He must have been a —— lunatic, Bob," said Mr. Ormsby, who had always gaped at the late minister as he would have gaped at a god, to Mr. Beebee, who had likewise gaped.

"It was so beastly ungentlemanly, Ormsby. I never did think there was much in him," rejoined Mr. Beebee.

"That's what I think, Bob; if he had been a gentleman he wouldn't have married her at all. I know if *I* had fancied the girl, *I* wouldn't. I'd have made her think it was all right."

"Of course you wouldn't have married her; it was devilish low. It makes me sick to think about it. I hope it wont be said that he was anything to me," put in Mr. Beebee, stretching himself. And then, because of the sickness that oppressed him, he went out to get rid of his nausea in the Park.

Those who had so long consorted with the minister cared nothing for the crime of his long desertion of his wife, but raved, as did Mr. Ormsby and Mr. Beebee, about the scandal of its getting exposed by being acknowledged.

This, and more like to it, was after many days the world's verdict upon Fabian Massareene; and even those who did not cast a stone, only so refrained themselves from casting, for the reason that they thought it were better such an one were clean forgotten.

But in certain drawing-rooms, that which he had done was not let to fade out of memory. The mother of the Lady Cecilia Carfax was minded to keep it always fresh.

"It is such a comfort for me to think that my Cecilia would not have him. Not one girl, Lady Langdale, in a thousand would have behaved as she did."

"So he said himself. He must have been a very bad man," replied Lady Langdale. "Now, how do you suppose he spoke

of your Cecilia?   He remarked to a friend
of mine that of course he had no intention
of making a proposal; but that it was a pity
you threw her at people, and that not one
girl in a thousand could make love as could
she.   Wasn't it shocking?"

"How wicked and indelicate!   And do
you know—I can hardly bear to tell you—
he said worse things about Feodore?   He
told me she was pretty, but pasty-looking,
and that he had thought you were too
much of a manager to have set her upon
him so conspicuously.   Isn't it almost
incredible?"

"It is quite incredible.   It could not
have been Feodore.   I—I—my girl has not
been out two seasons, or he might have
said it with some reason."   Now this had
been the second season with the Lady Cecilia,
and the mother of the Lady Cecilia
remembered that it was so, and was beaten
off.

In Black Moss only was the minister's
name not execrated, and the confession of
his guilt not reviled.   To the shocked and

disgusted critics, to the Ormsbys and the Beebees of the West End, it was, as has been shown, simply amazing and ungentlemanly that he should so have married such a girl at all; but that the marriage should not have been a false one, and the record of it on the registry a lie, was wholly inconceivable. The giving of her over to an open shame would have been a respectable and a usual thing to do. There were many precedents for that with which they were familiar. If there came to be an end to these *liaisons* there would come to be an end to society. "Why, there isn't a fellow, Beebee, who'd be safe," said Mr. Ormsby.

"There'd not be a gentleman left," shuddered out Mr. Beebee.

Now it had got to be known, that whilst Fabian Massareene had been that autumn time compassing the milk-maid with his many nets as Jasper Tudor, he had afterwards committed to her the secret of his name, and that by his own name they were married by license at Troutbeck church; for which purpose he had himself lived within

Troutbeck parish for the ten days next before their marriage, to the end that all might
be in order. Therefore, when it was told
what he had done, the amazed and silken
egotists at the clubs resented this as folly
so gratuitous and so immense, and so much
like to a designed reflection on themselves, that they felt moved to maintain
that they thought it to be only contemptible.
If he had proceeded to marry her to en-
courage some sentiment, and had afterwards
hidden her, they reasoned that the folly of
the sentiment would have been redeemed by
the common sense of the desertion. But
he, they insisted, might have held his peace
at the last. Because that he was dying it
was not required of him to commit a *bétise*.
There was nothing in the English tongue
that at all described the nature and extent
of the slip that he had made. He might
have done as it had pleased him, he might
have boasted of his bridal if they had not
known him. These moral obligations to
set forth everything, that always presented
themselves immediately before the death-

rattle, showed, as they put it, "so little re-
finement." They made it so inconvenient
for those who were left. Therefore, all that
they could say was. that they had never
known him, for if he had gone to his account
with a lie, his reputation as a gentleman, as
a man with refined and delicate tastes, would
not have suffered, but would have been sus-
tained; and as one who had desired their
acquaintance they had a right to demand
the consideration. And some of these had
lisped out just before, "Of course they'll
take him to the Abbey;" whilst others had
rejoined, "They ought to put him in S.
Paul's." So did those who once bowed
down before him now protest that they had
never bowed. And so did those who once
threw up their incense now cast up anathe-
mas.

Meanwhile, as these exquisites were in
this manner ashamed, and were proposing in
Pall Mall some unobjectionable forms to be
observed by a soul at its departure, the long
paralysed administration was only holding
on that its imbecility might not be con-

summated by the flinging away of any
patronage. A successor to Massareene, got
from an irreproachable family source, had
been found; and as the ministers avow-
edly had no programme, and were only
keeping their places until, in the mercy of
Parliament, they should be removed, if the
situation was not conspicuous for its dignity,
it was not without the compensation of
ease.

A considerable deanery, a deanery much
coveted by scholarly men, had been long pronounced to be one of the good things in the
gift of the Government, by reason of the
many infirmities of its aged holder: and
now was it that this good thing had to be
given away. It was early rumoured that
Guy Melchior would get it, as it was known
that Fabian Massareene, before he went
down to Black Moss, had warmly urged the
claims of the young vicar on the Premier.
But it was just because Guy Melchior's
patron had been the now extinguished
favourite, that each minister was prepared
to recommend some one of his own kin, for

the colleagues of the dead man were no truer to his memory than were the once parasites of the favourite throughout the country.

In the end the deanery went to an exceedingly finely proportioned person, a hunting man, a rowing man, a coursing man, and one who at times, it was said, could be also a cursing man. But then his family was such that it was not possible to pass him over; and had he not also on saints' days been always a little late getting to hounds? And so were those answered who presently said that such a dean was a terrible scandal. And *Bell's Life* fought for the new dean, and the manner of its fighting was this:—" It is quite time that the religious world should be told that there are some people with souls besides its own self-constituted members. A man who has rowed stroke-oar for his University, who has ridden to hounds for fifteen years, who has a leash of the best greyhounds in England, is not necessarily less godly than the man who has never sat in a boat, who has never been in a saddle, or who has never owned a dog. But we are reminded by some of our high Christian contemporaries that he has been heard to swear, and that he keeps bull-terriers. We are not going to ask whether the saints represented by our contemporaries have ever slipped with *their* tongues, but we know of no ecclesiastical law that provides a penalty for keeping bull-terriers. We may say that the Dean of S. Faith's has contributed many learned treatises upon the animals of Bible History. He is the author of a clever investigation with the title 'Did Nimrod wear pink?—but the work by which he will be recollected is "The substance and breeding of the horses that Noah took into the Ark." His sermons have many of them t rown much light upon these matters, and whilst one that we noticed in the spring upon the words, 'Grin like a dog,' shows a considerable knowledge of all the great kennels and best strains, yet, undoubtedly, it is exceeded in value by one lately preached, 'Dumb dogs that cannot bark.' In his work upon the

horses of the Ark, which is dedicated by per-
mission to the Veterinary College—he, we
think, conclusively shows that both the
horse and the mare were extraordinarily well
chosen; whilst in his two sermons he shows
the variety of 'grins' common among dogs,
and points out of what breed the 'dumb
dogs' probably were, with an illustration of
one of his own that never could give tongue.
The new dean is, we hear, declining hunting,
and his stud, which will be brought to the
hammer, will be removed next week from
the cathedral-yard."

Whilst the opposition journals published
his latest pamphlet upon "scent," and were
asking if the correct line to a deanery was
through the best seat in a saddle, the
Government organs made the announcement
judiciously unaccompanied with comment.
We shall not meet with the Dean of S.
Faith's again; therefore let it be said that
he parted with all his stud, even with his
favourite fencer; that he bought the cellar
of his predecessor; and that he only kept
such of his bull-terriers as did not fight.

There were, as has been shown, no stones cast at the memory of Fabian Massareene by any hand from Black Moss Abbey. Lady D'Aeth relaxed in none of her devotion to her who was now welcomed as Sybil, and the bruised Daisy was tenderly entreated at last to come home.

Now, Rooke, the butler, was a good deal concerned that no stones were thrown. As Wauchope had disclosed, he had not found a shop, but he held certain of the prerogatives of the pantry in high regard, and one of these prerogatives was, that co-equal with the perquisites of such a situation was its dignity. And he who was not accustomed to the disparagement of his office, got to be of opinion that in the interest of all chief butlers it would ill comport with his representative position to set meat before one who had at any time milked cows; therefore he concluded that he ought to go.

"Please, my lady, can I speak to your ladyship for a minute?" inquired Rooke one morning, as he was sweeping the crumbs from the breakfast-table.

"You can speak now, Rooke, said Lady D'Aeth. "What is it you wish to say?" And she put down the book that she was reading, and Rooke gracefully arranged his napkin under his arm, and came round the table.

"You see, my lady, of course I's got a hexellent character, and Lord Sussex said he never did see such a way as I had for drawing a cork out of port-wine. I isn't in nowise afeared about a character; but though I isn't going into another place, my lady, I can't come down, and I'd wish to leave when your ladyship's sooted."

" Rooke, I do not like my servants to have any just ground of complaint against me. I hope you are not leaving because you are not comfortable?"

" I isn't comfortable in my mind, my lady. I can't wait on that young person. I can't carry plates to any one who isn't genteel, who's milked cows. I——"

" There; you have said too much already, Rooke; I do not wish to hear any more."

" I 'ope I hasn't given no offence, my lady;

but I hasn't been used to mixed society; I's
very partic'lar. I should drop the dishes
some day; I know I should. Why, she ain't
fit to touch Wauchope nohow, my lady.
She——"

And Rooke was ordered out, and he left
the Abbey that afternoon—as he never was
afterwards forgetful to say—covered with
all his honour."

Whilst Rooke had been so superbly re-
senting the indignity offered to his office,
Black Moss had not been in any way for-
getting Gideon Cuyp.

By some it had been endeavoured to show
that the undertaker was not guilty of those
things with which his memory was charged.
But one by one these fell away, and presently
there were none who could make answer to
those who witnessed of the dead man's crimes.

Now Job Redcar's suspicion had not
wasted. Little by little it had come on,
waxing every day, until, in the end, it was
sitting upon most in the place, with all
those shapes in the which it sat upon the
swiller. And the further such investi-

gations were worked and pushed, so much the blacker did the undertaker's memory get to be.

It so chanced that some of the amazing powder with which Gideon Cuyp had soothed so many mourners had had violent hands laid on it, when its destructive properties at last got that recognition which had been so long accorded to its protective virtues. That powder, for which not a few had offered their all, was a fraud—more than all his other frauds. That infamous specific, for which he had extorted so great a number of pounds, was found to have no corresponding value even in pence. After this had got to be known his other distinctions were not troubled with any test. All that he had ever done was now taken to have been only full of evil. His charities, his drugs, his alms, were all alike pronounced to be accursed; only because of Sybil were they satisfied with any measure of execration that did not demand the mutilation of his body. But for her it would not have rested in its grave. But then for her they would have done much more than let the clay alone.

From papers that were, after a long search, found hidden away in his cottage, it appeared that Gideon Cuyp had left behind him a great gathering of gold, and had not Job Redcar thrown oil upon the waters, the house would have been burned and the money-bags seized. They who had come about it cried out that the gold was covered with the blood of their wives and of their little ones ; and hardly could the swiller persuade them not to lay their hands upon it; for it was not now forgotten that he who had left behind him all this substance had gotten it out of their desolation. Neither had it gone out of their minds that he who had so filled these bags was none other than he who had murmured about his small profits, and had lied about his losses, telling to them, the while, that the laying up of treasure here was not a thing in which his soul delighted. Therefore did they come threateningly about the house in the which it had been garnered, and cry that they would burn it. Neither did it seem to be well with them, when it got to be understood that it was chiefly by the stripping of those who were left for ever naked by the stripping, that he had filled these bags. It was not possible, indeed, to bring certain things which were alleged against him home. They had not been contrived to be found out by the master mind of Gideon Cuyp. In the beginning, just after the undertaker had been buried, some had hesitated to believe that, under the mask of much pretended benevolence, he should have so left a fevered coat to do its work in the house of Guy Melchior. But then it was also quite sufficiently shown that he knew the cloth must be infected. And one of those who at the first did not feel assured about the undertaker's guilt was Lady D'Aeth.

"I cannot persuade myself, Mr. Melchior, to think with those who say these things against him. I cannot see the motive that he could have had."

"I am afraid it is true, Lady D'Aeth; but I would the rather not say what I think.

Let us forget that we ever knew him. He need not now be judged of us."

"But if it was as you believe Mr. Melchior, what could have been his motive for desiring your life?"

"That, Lady D'Aeth, I cannot tell you now. I have buried his body; suffer me, also, to bury his memory. God grant that I am wrong; but I am not wrong; I *know* he did desire it."

"And may not I, who have taken that man's child to be my own—may not I, Mr. Melchior, ask to be told why you so suspect him?"

"Lady D'Aeth, I struggled long against believing it myself; but it was too strong for me. If I speak to you of it now, have I your promise that you will never call it back to me again?"

· You have that promise, Mr. Melchior."

Then he came round and bent over Lady D'Aeth, and whispered in her ear—

" Because he thought that Sybil loved me." And after he had so spoken, he went out.

Taken also with his last words to the vicar

on the evening of the flood, it got to be clear to most in Black Moss that Gideon Cuyp's was the hand that shut those gates and let the waters of the tarn upon them. And taken with the now detected worthlessness of the marvellous powder, which he purveyed at so great a price, and with the later finding out of so much gold, after so many protestations of emptiness, Job Redcar did not in the end find it to be hard to bring Black Moss over to his suspicion.

"We'll nit mel* ov his brass," said Job to the big miner on that day when it had been almost resolved to burn the undertaker's house and take his bags. .

"An' we'll nit kindle a fire, Job; he's likely warrm enoo wie t'dulet at hell."

"Ay, ay, Job," said many more, who had come there to light a fire. "Ye's happen reet ; Cuyp's wie t'dule, an' gae warrm yonder wie a deal er spurrits akin ta he." And so they were comforted because of what the undertaker was pronounced to be.

And after then it was that that which was

* Meddle.　　　 † The devil.

T 2

told of Gideon Cuyp in the valley began to
spread.   It reached the people on the fells;
it reached the statesmen on the passes
round; it reached into every corner of the
county.   From the north it presently came
south, and, in the end, it reached to London.
There the chief journals were for some days
filled with the latest particulars concerning
"the Black Moss mystery;" and those prints
that were of the best repute for special intelligence, and for being reliable, sent their
reporters up to Cumberland; therefore the
fortunes of Black Moss did not look to be
mending.   It had gotten a bad name, and it
could not cast it off.   Those who had gone
there to fish in its streams were minded that
they would not go there to fish again; so
a thick gloom sat upon the place, shutting
up the Fish Inn, and otherwise making itself
felt; and whilst Job Redcar's suspicion was
so aired, in the columns even of the *Times*,
there were those who had not ceased to talk
about it when Parliament assembled.

In the first fortnight of that February
there came to be a ministerial crisis; the

Government, after a three nights' debate, was left in a large minority, and the supporters of the Cabinet were thrown upon their remarkable resources in intrigue to get back to the Treasury Bench on some pretentious pretext, or on some *ad captandum* pledge.

It was about this time that Guy Melchior was in many ways and in various forms receiving the marked regard of those who, strangers to him, nevertheless had read of his escape, and had heard of his services. The offer to present him to livings, exceeding in value only by a very little his own, had been made to him by certain patrons whom he had never seen, but who desired to remove him out of the reach of the waters; for they felt that their sympathies were with the man whose life had been these two times so preserved.

Now it may be truly said, that the Vicar of Black Moss did, however, desire no preferment, for the sake of a money advantage, that so he might get more to eat and more to drink. Guy Melchior was neither so hungry nor so thirsty but that he could live upon that which he had. He did not seek to be preferred because things might so be made to him a little easier. But if he could have been so advantaged that he might, with independence, have been able to address Sybil Massareene, then he would have been persuaded to go up higher. Guy Melchior did not take himself to be a desirable investment for a well-dowered girl. He had heard it said by priests and deacons that they were otherwise so favoured that they need not be well found in the things of this world, to seek for an abundance of the good things of this world in their wives. He had seen many orders of pastors laying themselves out to marry for money, some with one art and some with another : some with small talk, some with their smiles, some with their sermons, some with their eyes, holding alone this one doctrine in common, that the office of a clergyman is so spiritual that even the pauper priest bears about in his profession a richer possession than any fortune in the funds. Now Guy Melchior believed the spiritual riches of his office to be one thing, and a fortune in the funds to be another; and he did not mean to say to any girl, "My riches are not of this world, your riches are—suffer them, therefore, to be joined together, and so let them be shared by us both."

Events had of late brought the vicar and Sybil once more into closer companionship; but he did not think that much closer companionship would be for his own peace. He persuaded himself that she had not ceased to love him; but, then, such preferment as had been offered of late would not have given him the right to ask of her her love. To the sweetness and loveliness of Sybil a fortune that was splendid would presently be added. To that which he had, so far as he knew, would presently be added nothing; therefore, Guy Melchior reasoned that he might not, as a true man, entreat of her to have him.

The money left behind by Gideon Cuyp had passed to Edith Massareene, who, notwithstanding that their relations were very remote, was yet his nearest of kin, and to

Sybil would presently come down the fortune of her mother. Guy Melchior feeling
within himself that his claims to her love
were none the less likely to succeed with
her because of what he had not, would
nevertheless do nothing to her prejudice.
So the vicar now, the rather, avoided Sybil,
lest he might fall away, as he had fallen
away before, and lest he should be persuaded to tell to her that which within himself he could so hardly control. To the
questionings of Lady D'Aeth and of Sybil,
why he continued to refuse the livings that
were offered to him, he made answer that
he did not desire to be leaving Black Moss
for another hundred pounds a-year; and it
is only likely that but for Sybil he would
have gone on refusing everything that would
have taken him from her.

Lady D'Aeth, however, assured herself
that in this matter the vicar ought to be
advised.

"I think I never saw a man care so little
about money as you do, Mr. Melchior. It
almost makes it hard to believe you are a
clergyman."

"I care about money a great deal more than you suppose, Lady D'Aeth," replied the vicar, smiling; "yet I would not give up my friends here for a hundred pounds a-year."

"But you would give them up for hundreds, eh, Mr. Melchior?" laughed Lady D'Aeth.

"I might, Lady D'Aeth, have that with many hundreds which I may not ask to have with one."

"And pray what is that, Mr. Melchior?" But when Lady D'Aeth looked up, the vicar had escaped into the garden, and there was nothing left but that on Sybil's face which told to Lady D'Aeth how matters were. Some time she had suspected how they were, but now was she very sure.

In the March of that year it was that the Dean of S. Chad's fell sick and died. The sensitive critics of the party in power were greatly concerned lest there should be a scandal to the Church, and lest the administration should give that very considerable thing to any one without such parts as would beseem a dean. The names of several divines, some hungry, some patient, some expectant and lofty, some expecting nothing, and meek, were announced in turn as likely to succeed Dr. Cupples at S. Chad's; but those of the hungry and the patient, the lofty and the meek, whose names and claims had been paraded, were none of them chosen for the great good thing ; and the *Times*, at last, put an end to the hopes of the lofty, and to the fears of the meek, by this declaration of the choice of the administration :— "We understand that the deanery of S. Chad's has been offered to the Rev. Guy Melchior, Vicar of Black Moss, Cumberland, and that it has been accepted by him. Mr. Melchior, as a parish priest, has long shown his fitness for the higher office to which he is now preferred, and we believe it is to this, rather than to any other circumstances in his career, which have lately been made public, that the Government has well concluded to nominate Mr. Melchior to the vacant deanery."

It was one evening when the Vicar of

Black Moss had bethought himself that he would go down to the Abbey, that the offer of this preferment was put into his hands. After he had read the letter, he was the more resolved to go and tell them about this matter there; and then if Sybil Massareene should seem to desire him to take it, he was already minded that he would not refuse. The deanery of S. Chad's was worth more than ten hundred pounds a-year, and the Dean of S. Chad's was also more than ten times greater than the Vicar of Black Moss. And thinking this thing over to himself, he thought that he might the more fitly now speak to Sybil; so he went down to the Abbey about the time of the serving of the tea.

"Lady D'Aeth," he said, after that the tea had been taken away; " I have come here to-night to ask you to advise with me. I have had a letter—will you give me your advice?"

. " A letter, Mr. Melchior, asking to know of your intentions? Sybil, my darling, put down your work, the vicar is going to be

married. If it is about a wife, Mr. Melchior," said Lady D'Aeth, laughing, " I
say to you at once, don't hesitate; clergymen ought to marry, for I am sure I may
assume that you would not give your affections
to any one unworthily. Sybil, do not get
behind that work; the vicar is going to tell
us all about the lady."

Guy Melchior who, whilst Lady D'Aeth
was speaking, had glanced at Sybil and had
seen the blush which covered her face, began
to feel it to be hard to make answer to this
interpretation of that which he had said, but
bowing to the compliment, he replied very
seriously, " No, Lady D'Aeth, I have had
no such letter. I have not been asked about
my intentions; it is not that; I—I sometimes think that I shall never marry."

" Then, Mr. Melchior, you are not like
most other clergymen I know. They seem
to think that they have only got to ask and
to have. I once heard one solemnly declare
he thought a clergyman, with a proper
regard for his office, ought not to marry
below the daughter of an earl. But if it is

not about a wife, what can it be that I am
to advise on ?"

"Well, then, it is about becoming a dean.
I have just been offered the deanery of S.
Chad's."

"Was there ever quite so lucky a man as
our vicar, Sybil?" said Lady D'Acth, reading
the letter. "Of course you will accept this,
Mr. Melchior; but you will have some
work upon your hands coming after Dr.
Cupples. Ask Sybil about it, she is quite
an authority in these things."

"Auntie, I don't know any deans."

"Why, it was only last evening, Sybil,
that you told me the deanery of S. Chad's
ought to be given to Mr. Melchior. I won't
tell you what else she said; it was not very
bitter. But I cannot stay now; there is
poor Mrs. Dibbs that I must see to-night."
And then she went out, leaving the other
two together.

Now the vicar did not sigh or make a
speech, or otherwise deport himself after the
manner of heroes; but when Sybil Massareene looked up from her work, he was

standing by her side, and presently it seemed as if he had put his arm about her, and then she heard him say, "Tell me, darling, what shall I do? It is for you to give an answer to this letter, for I cannot leave this place without you. Sybil, I told you once that I would never ask you to become my wife; that you should never hear of my love again; and to that I would have tried to have been true, if it had not been for this that has come to me to-night. The Vicar of Black Moss, Sybil, had only his love, the Dean of S. Chad's ———"

He would have gone on, but that he was stayed by a beseeching look from her earnest eyes—"Oh, it is not that! it is not that! I have always loved you only, Guy."

"Then, Sybil, I may ask of you that which I said I would never ask of you again. Answer me here—here, on my heart, Sybil. Answer me now."

And she did answer him there. And "You may ask me, Guy," was all she said.

CHAPTER IX.

IN THE GAP.

EARLY the next morning Guy Melchior presented himself at the Abbey to ask of Lady D'Aeth her consent, for under her care Sybil still in reality remained by the wish of Edith Massareene.

The vicar believed that most women. in a situation of such delicate trust must have their own views concerning how their charges ought to marry. He remembered to have heard that it was a prerogative dear to womankind to order this great matter; and it had also been told him that even the mildest of gentlewomen would not suffer that any one should come upon this ground. And it might be that Lady D'Aeth had taken up ground on the which she meant that Sybil Massareene should stand.

So Guy Melchior did not feel to be assured about the answer he would get. He was persuaded that Lady D'Aeth had probably her views upon the marrying of Sybil— strong views that it would, perhaps, be scarcely safe to seek to overset. She had probably some alliance in her own mind that she might have set herself upon cementing. The vicar had heard of that one who had a thousand pounds a-day, and of those others who had come about Sybil, offering to give to her all their love and all their inheritance. And it might be that Lady D'Aeth was yet resolved on Sybil marrying one of these. Guy Melchior had heard how the daughter of Massareene had sent away men with fortunes even more remarkable than were their pedigrees or their persons. It might be that Lady D'Aeth was not well pleased that they should have so been sent away, and was minded that Sybil ought to choose from amongst them. He did not think but that he stood well with Sybil's aunt; but then he was not like to those who had come so thickly round about

the child of the fallen favourite ; and he remembered that whilst he had none of their
substance he had also none of their ways. And
then it must be said that the vicar had not
been that long time so well affected towards
himself, and so assured of his success, as
to think that Sybil Massareene had said she
would not have those millions, and would
not be joined to that blood, because of him.
After that he had so grievously slipped
that afternoon, when he had fallen away
from his purpose not to speak, and had
spoken of his great love under the beeches,
he had meant that that which was in him
should never again so move him; and
afterwards he had not further inquired of
his heart if the daughter of Massareene still
held to her love. Therefore it was only
her words to him of the night before, " I have
always loved you *only*, Guy," that now
brought him to see how enduringly, and
faithfully, and with what strength he had
been preferred, whilst every temptation to
forget him glittered before her. Nevertheless, as he had thought that night through,

Lady D'Aeth might be otherwise concerned to dispose of Sybil. So it was with some fears as to the answer he would get, that he forsook his breakfast and set out early for the Abbey.

Now Lady D'Aeth was not minded how she would order the marrying of Sybil Massareene. She loved the gentle girl with all her heart, and she desired nothing but that Sybil should be well loved of a true man. She knew something concerning the chief symptoms of these things, and she had sometimes thought that she could see how this matter with the vicar was going on. The interest that Sybil took in Guy Melchior's work in that place might be quite likely not unexplained by her strong sympathy for the Church's cause: but then it was also not wholly impossible that it should be in a measure stimulated by other regards. She had seen how Sybil had answered to those who had come about her, and she had been amazed at that which she saw. It was to her, for a time, a thing that was hard to be understood; but now she

thought that she could understand it. She
had had her views like as have most women.
Yet had she not pushed them according to
the fashion of womankind.

Lady D'Aeth was purposed to leave to
Sybil all that she possessed, so that the real
choice of Sybil's heart need not be in any way
affected by Guy Melchior's means. She had,
she could remember, seen "great matches"
in the loftiest places, as the correctest critics
pronounced them to be, where the fortunes
on both sides were excellently well balanced,
and where there were no contrasts at all in
the weight of the purses, with some after
results that she did not at all desire should
come into any of Sybil's experiences. She
had seen these marriages of inexorable con-
venience; she had heard the vows go up
where she knew there were hearts recoiling
from the perjury that joined together the
best bloo and made the highest houses
happy. She did not desire that Sybil should
be joined to blood, or that she should bear
a noble name, or succeed to great possessions, upon any of these terms. She did

not mean that Sybil should be taken up so high only that she might presently break her heart in the midst of that glory which would be to her a desolation; therefore she resolved that Guy Melchior should be heard, if it might be that he desired to speak. Nevertheless, Lady D'Aeth had sometimes thought that the vicar had not as yet concluded what he would do in this matter. He did not seem to her as one who was eager in his love; yet she was not sure but that his love was eager, only that he had held it back because he feared, with the little that he had, to ask in marriage this queenly girl who had so much. But whilst she had rightly determined what were the motives of Guy Melchior's hesitation, she could not, however, charge her memory with having seen in any places many such scruples holding back the great company of vicars or curates, with no more sufficient incomings than had the Vicar of Black Moss, but who by their blandishments, both in the pulpit and out of it, in church and at Chiswick, seemed to be setting their affections on heiresses with more fer-

vour than on the things of heaven. So she
was slow to understand what Guy Melchior
had it in his mind to do.

Now Sybil Massareene had said nothing
to her aunt of that which had been asked of
her by the vicar, or of how she had answered
him, the night before ; Guy Melchior having
persuaded her that it would be more seemly
and regular if he first told Lady D'Aeth of
this matter himself. So it was agreed that
he should come up to the Abbey early the
next morning.

"I am afraid your aunt may not see fit
to give you to me, Sybil," the vicar had said
before they parted.

" Then you don't know auntie if you think
so, Guy. She only wants me to be happy ;
so of course she will see fit to give me to
you."

Therefore her last words had in a measure
brought comfort to the vicar.

" Well, Mr. Melchior," said Lady D'Aeth,
smiling, as Guy awkwardly and nervously
got himself into the room, and fidgeted
round a chair, " and so Sybil tells me you

have made up your mind to take the deanery."

" Yes—that is—Sybil—I mean Miss Massareene—thought I had better, and you told me to ask her about it; and I would wish to take it, Lady D'Aeth; but if you will, you can decide the matter for me."

And then the vicar came round the chair, and sat him down upon it. He was not at his ease, and he could not help showing how it was with him. He could not act a part; he would not have known how to set about it. He was not sure but that Lady D'Aeth would begin to laugh when he began to speak; so he did many things with his body that it were better he should not have done; and he knew that in his confusion he only demeaned himself awkwardly.

" Then I decide now," said Lady D'Aeth, trying to help the vicar out of his difficulties, and to put him at his ease; " so that I may salute you at once as Dean of S. Chad's. Therefore you see it is all settled, Mr. Melchior."

Guy Melchior knew that his time was

come; he also knew that his brain seemed to swim, and that that which he would say would also seem to be swimming; but the words that leaped to his lips were true words, even if their leaping was a little wild, as he answered, "I will go to S. Chad's, Lady D'Aeth, if you will let me take Sybil there as my wife. I will love her and cherish her." And then he said, with terrible earnestness, as he saw a smile upon the face of Lady D'Aeth, "Tell me to be gone, if I have asked of you too much, but do not laugh, for my love is very true."

"I could not laugh, Mr. Melchior; but you must let me show that I am glad. I should not tell you all that I felt, if I did not say that I could only bear, I think, to lose her that she might become yours. For her mother's consent, I am permitted to answer. She always hoped it might be so." And then she came up to the vicar, and he felt that her tears were dropping on his hand. "Neither do I fear that Sybil will refuse to go," she presently went on to say. "But was it not last night that you told us, very gravely, you perhaps should never marry?"

"My dear Lady D'Aeth, that was because I did not know, then, that Sybil would have taken me."

"Then, Mr. Melchior, let me say, you could scarcely have seen as others have. I myself believed, when Sybil, this spring, was so cold and indifferent to addresses that most girls would have sought, and that very few would have rejected, that her heart was occupied, and so I wrote to Gideon Cuyp. I hoped then, and I have hoped through all, that it would come to this. She is almost as dear to me as the lost one was, and in this welcome to you as a son, I do thank God for my darling's choice. Yes, Guy, you may do it," for the vicar had been plunging round about her hand as if he could scarcely persuade himself to take it up and kiss it, whilst she had been speaking.

"Dear, dear aunt," said Sybil, who had just come in, and had already seen something of the situation, "you *will* let me love him, you are calling him Guy—but you are crying, you mustn't cry about it, auntie."

"I cannot, sweet one, help these tears, because I am so very happy, Sybil. I think that he whom you have chosen is not un-worthy of my darling; and I need not tell you, Guy, anything about *your* prize, I think."

"The vicar, aunt," said Sybil, archly, " knows very well that I am only a weak wilful little thing; now, don't you?" And then she took him by the coat and pulled him coaxingly towards her aunt; "And I want you, mister sir, to promise to let me have my way at once; you mustn't be a hard man yet."

" Well, I don't think I will be hard with you this time, I'll not try to check your wilful symptoms, Sybil, yet. What is it I am to promise?"

" Why, to make this precious aunt of ours—for you know she is yours now— come very often to see us at S. Chad's, and never to let her say no, when we ask her."

"Lady D'Aeth,——"

"I am your aunt, sir, if you please; did not you hear that young lady's order?"

"Well then, my good aunt, you will have to sit in Mrs. Dean's place in the cathedral very often indeed. I shall never get to believe that Sybil is the less yours because she is mine."

After this little speech of the vicar's, Sybil and her aunt went into each other's arms, and had a cry. And it were better said there was a little skirmishing between their smiles and their tears, and the affair was left a drawn one.

"Then there is nothing more to settle, I suppose," said Lady D'Aeth; after which she added, with much mock gravity, "You are not in any haste to leave me, Sybil?"

"I suppose I must learn to do as I am told at once, aunt. Please to ask Guy."

"There is your mother, Sybil, I have yet to ask. Your aunt has said that Mrs. Massareene thinks well of me. Yet it is her due that I should speak to her about it."

"I am sure that the vicar is right," said Lady D'Aeth.

"Auntie," murmured Sybil, " did you ever know him to be wrong?"

In the end when Edith Massareene returned to the Abbey, it was resolved they should be married some time in the next autumn. The many and the grievous accusations that rested against Gideon Cuyp had been with much kindly forethought kept from the knowledge of Sybil; and although she had heard that he had not been her uncle, his memory was none the less dear and sacred to her. Fabian Massareene—her father for one day—had died in the August, so that if their marriage was set down for the September in the year to come, there would be twelvemonths between that celebration and her father's death.

Edith Massareene, although not at the Abbey when Guy Melchior had so asked of Sybil to become his wife, had nevertheless made haste to get back when she had been told by Lady D'Aeth of what was done, and confessed to Guy with full eyes, and a fuller

heart, that the sorrows of her life would be
no longer remembered.

"Sen th'* day he left ma I's nivver hed
sick a joy as this; ye'll nit be leavin' oor
conny Sybil. I raiken † ye'll nit be gettin'
quit er her, ye'll nivver slat ‡ her at cauld
world ?"

"I am not fit that she should love me,
Mrs. Massareene; but, God helping me, I
will be very true," and that was all that
ever passed between them concerning that
matter.

Excepting such few familiars as had come
about her during the many years of that
terrible forsakening, Edith Massareene had
had no other hope this side the grave, than
that Sybil's future should be nothing like to
her own. She was almost fearful that Sybil
should ever come to give her love lest it
also should be betrayed; lest she also should
be listening to words as pleasant and as
soft as once had been the words of Jasper
Tudor. She feared lest a fisher should
look upon her child; for the lessons of her

* Siuce the.   † Think.   ‡ Throw.

life had scarcely left to her the heart with which to trust again. But if her faith in that which could not lie had not died out, then she felt that she might give it to the vicar.

Lady D'Aeth had told her of the attachment she suspected that there was between Sybil and Guy Melchior, and even in so short a time she had got to see that, in the manner of his life, he was not like to other men, and that it was such that even Sybil's love might, without fearing, shine upon; for, as Edith had come to know the vicar better, and could see how well he walked, she, in the end, had got to set her hopes on such a one, walking, his life through, by the side of her child. And so she had journeyed back with haste to tell to the vicar of all her faith in him, and all she felt.

Therefore, as Lady D'Aeth had said, everything was settled and concluded concerning the wedding; it having been determined that they should be married at the church of Black Moss. But as Guy Melchior would have to go before the time of

their being married into residence at the
Deanery, neither he nor Sybil could be comforted concerning this affecting separation;
for Guy, now that he was getting to be
bolder, could speak out much as did other
men. Not that his mouth was filled with
foolishness, or that the manner of his speech,
now that he had won, was more frivolous
than it had been whilst he wooed, yet he
did none of the awkward things which, with
his body, he had done before; and with a
better grace he made his love.

Then there was a great deal to be done
in the way of getting the marriage things,
and only a few months to get them in.
There was apparel to be bought, and in the
buying of the wedding garment womankind
will not be hastened.

Lady D'Aeth, whose heart was in this
matter that there was between the vicar
and Sybil, resolved that it should be in the
shopping also, and that her sympathies and
her purse should work together. She,
therefore, beyond the other gifts of silks and
linen, for which she made herself responsible,

was also set on furnishing the Deanery, so that, as she put it, she might be afterwards sufficiently excused if she should come to see how the upholstery was wearing.

Guy had now got himself away from Black Moss, and the energies of the new dean were already beginning to take hold of S. Chad's. Now, Dr. Cupples, whom he succeeded, had been an amiable, a weak, and a bending man. So far also as the getting of the good things of the church went, Dr. Cupples had been always getting them abundantly. In his earlier days he had lighted upon his legs, in the parish of the Right Hon. Thomas Peploe, a Privy Councillor, and a Protestant who ran at the scarlet lady, as does a bull at red cloth. He had been some time a widower, and was joined in his exercises against the scarlet abominations by his only child, Cornelia. Cornelia Peploe was forty-two when Mr. Cupples came as a curate to Peploedown, and when he first went up to the great man's house, to be turned over, she made a maidenly resolve that she would have him. So when the vicar died, Mr.

Cupples went into the vicarage, and was made chaplain to the Privy Councillor. He knew that by Cornelia's favour he had been brought up to this high ground. He knew that she took notes of his sermons; he knew that the little things in lawn, which came to him, were of her sewing and her sending; and he also knew that the Privy Councillor could set him higher than he was already set; therefore, when Cornelia was getting to be forty-three, Mr. Cupples put to her a question, and she, believing that virginity was abhorred of Rome, consented to be taken from her father's house. Then the Deanery of S. Chad's fell in, and the Peploe interest was such that Mr. Cupples got it.

The dean had been bidden by his wife to make a great contention for " pure Protestantism," and terribly had waxed the strife between the lady and the chapter.

Now, it has been said that Dr. Cupples was an amiable and a bending man; and it must also be told that Mrs. Cupples knew it. Mrs. Cupples in her time had managed Peploedown; and when she went to S.

Chad's it was on her mind that she would also manage the cathedral; and Dr. Cupples, when he had been in residence a week, after this sort got to see that verily and, indeed, his wife would be the dean. She would have Tate and Brady, and she protested she would not have the little boys in white.

" Doctor Cupples, they say they will sing it, and I say they shan't—have you seen this wicked Popish hymn?"

And so Mrs. Cupples came into the presence of the dean, and cast down before him some crumpled papers she had carried from the choir.

Now, the dean knew what happened to him when he was so inquired of by his wife as Doctor Cupples. He knew that her Protestant vigour was stirred, and that too suddenly he might not stop her.

"No, my dear, I——"

"Doctor Cupples, I have not done yet—they are singing Popish songs —'Hold Thou Thy cross before my closing eyes.' Doctor Cupples, no one shall hold a cross before my eyes—nor before yours, nor before

the eyes of any one else in this place—are
we in a Protestant country, answer me that?
Is this a Protestant Cathedral? I—I wish
that I had never left papa. Why don't you
say something against these Jesuits? It
will end in your going over, I know it will
—but this infamous hymn shall not be
sung."

"But, my dear——"

"Doctor Cupples, I will have no buts. I
am only a weak woman, and you have
deceived me——"

"*I*, Mrs. Cupples?"

"Yes, sir, when you took me away from
papa, you said you were such a Protestant;
and now you seem to have forgotten it was
I who made of you a dean."

Now, Mrs. Cupples by this saying meant
to make reference to that exceeding influence
of her family which had carried Dr. Cupples
up; and it just also a little ruffled up the
dean.

"My dear, this constant referring to your
services is not nice—you are not generous."

"Dr. Cupples, you are a poor thing—you

are like a wave of the sea that is driven of the winds and tossed."

"Cornelia! this is not becoming of *my* Cornelia. I am not like a wave of the sea : I know where to *make* a stand—I cannot consent to make myself ridiculous."

"You had better order some dolls and other idols to be set up at once, Doctor Cupples."

"I will not let you make me angry, Cornelia; but I cannot interfere about these hymns."

"Then I *will* interfere, Dr. Cupples. Do you think that I will have a horrid cross dangling before my eyes ?"

"I am afraid, Cornelia, that I cannot help your being foolish, if you will be so."

"Now you are in a passion, Dr. Cupples— you are calling me names. I will write to papa, and I *will* interfere."

And it was the experience of the chapter, of the vicars choral, and of others at S. Chad's that if the dean did not interfere about the hymns, yet Mrs. Cupples did. So it may be seen to what confusion and what strifes

the Vicar of Black Moss succeeded at
S. Chad's.

After that Guy Melchior had gone into
residence, Lady D'Aeth and Sybil made
many journeys over to the Deanery to settle
some niceties in the colours and shades of
the decorations; and there was soon nothing
more to do but to deal with the great and
the delicate bridesmaid question. The dean
was for being married without any proces-
sion of young ladies, and he said so; but
having so said he was able to learn that he
had not minded his own business.

Not only had it to be agreed how these
young ladies should be apparelled, but what
was of infinitely greater concern, how many
those young ladies should be.

Again the dean was of opinion that if
there must be a crowd, it had better be a little
one; but Lady D'Aeth, who meant to give
the dresses, would not hear him further in
the matter. It was not found to be hard to
get five of one age and stature; but it so
happened that it was very hard to find a
sixth of any sort.

The enthusiasm which is incidental to this honourable office is in a measure limited when it is announced that "the wedding is to be very quiet." Moreover, young ladies who are not in any way opposed to taking a part in a pageant in veils, are not nearly so well satisfied to assist at a tame and tepid ceremonial where they are required to wear bonnets. And Guy Melchior felt within himself that he was glad a sixth could not be found; but when there got to be this perplexity in the councils at Black Moss, it was that Sybil herself came to the rescue.

"Aunt, I know you will not think me to be right; but do let me ask Feodore Mount-trevor."

Lady D'Aeth could only laugh at this which she heard; she had not at first the power to answer this appeal in words, but at last she tried to say, "Feodore Mount-trevor be one of *your* bridesmaids, Sybil?"

"I mean it, aunt. I am sure she would."

"My darling, your innocence and faith

are amazing. Feodore Mounttrevor be any one's bridesmaid to wear a bonnet! My love, you must surely have forgotten how she treated you this spring, and how that excellent Lady Langdale behaved to me."

"I have tried to forget it, aunt; but then I have not tried to forget that Feodore said at Lady Windermere's ball how sorry she was for what she had done, and that she would not hate me any more. I am sure she will come if you will let me ask her."

"Oh, you may ask her, Sybil; and a very pretty little letter I think I shall be getting from her mother."

So the Lady Feodore Mounttrevor was asked to be bridesmaid to Sybil Massareene, and she went straight to Lady Langdale, and she said, "Sybil Massareene is going to be married to the Dean of S. Chad's, and wants me to be one of her bridesmaids. Mamma, I should like to be one very much, may I?"

"No, Feodore, you may certainly not. I am exceedingly displeased that you should have asked me. What can you be thinking of? The nasty, bold thing. *I* know who *I* am."

" But, mamma——"

"Silence, I will not be answered; I was going to observe that perhaps the impudent girl who has so presumed as to write this letter does not know of which of her father's infamous loves she comes. *You* to walk behind the— the—there, I don't know what to call her— she'd push herself in anywhere. Feodore, you've quite upset me. Her mother's father kept a cow and took in single gentlemen; and this is the girl who flaunts about London for a season, making eyes at every one, and whom no one would notice but a silly clergyman; who went to the May Drawing-room, and to the Queen's Ball instead of sitting at home upon her milk-ing-stool. And the painted thing dares to write to you to come to the wedding of a milkmaid. Feodore, I am shocked and grieved that you should have asked me."

" And I, mamma, am very grieved that you should be so bitter. We were very cruel

to her, and I told her at Lady Windermere's
ball that we were very sorry——"

"Feodore—you dared—you——"

"I told her I quite loved her—for——"

"Feodore, leave the room; I will not hear
you—you have disgraced us. I will tell
Lady D'Aeth that if ever that milkmaid
dares——"

"Mamma, Sybil Massareene does not
milk cows; she never did; and if——"

"And if she did, I suppose you would not
think it beneath you to know her. Say no
more, child; I will not be spoken to. Go
to your room directly. I am exceedingly
displeased. I shall write to Lady D'Aeth;
and I insist that you will take no notice of
that impudent little mynx's letter."

And Feodore Mounttrevor went up to
her room, and she gently wrote to Sybil
why she could not come. Lady Langdale also went to write to Lady D'Aeth,
and this was the letter that she presently
had written :—

"Lady Langdale presents her compliments

to Lady D'Aeth, and has been excessively
surprised at a letter which a young person
has written to Lady Feodore Mounttrevor,
from Lady D'Aeth's house. Lady Langdale
knows nothing of this person who has taken
so great a liberty, beyond that which is now
notorious—that her mother was in the
milk trade, and had relations with the late
Mr. Massareene. Lady Langdale must beg
it to be understood that this is not a connexion that she desires for the Lady Feodore
Mounttrevor."

"There, Sybil, it is as I told you it would
be," said Lady D'Aeth; " but never mind,
darling, she cannot make me angry, and I
do not regret that you should have written,
since Feodore has answered you so kindly."
So the letter was torn up, and after that it
was not again spoken of between them.

The difficulty concerning the sixth bridesmaid was otherwise got over, and Sybil
Massareene and Guy Melchior were married
at the old church of S. Wilfred's, Black
Moss, about the time of barley harvest. It
was a fresh and a beautiful autumn day, and

not only from the valley and the fells, from the gap, and from Red Moss, but from places and passes that were far away, came the glad and the honest folk to see and to salute those who had been joined together.

They passed the first month of their married life at Ullswater and Windermere—at Ullswater, in that little cottage, in the which Sybil had been born. Then Edith Massareene went with them to the Deancry; and by Christmas they were all once more, for a little season, at Black Moss Abbey.

It was on the night before they were leaving to go back to S. Chad's that Job Redcar came to see the dean. The swiller had been mending his ways ever since the day that he got up from his sick bed, for so had the vicar's words been blessed that they had taken hold.

"There's bin a gae mash oop, Meester Melchior, sen thy bawn* frae Black Moss— t' parson's weel enoo, bet he's nowt akin ta ya—there's a deeal er new lights an' screamers as coom ta shout a Soondays; t' spot 'll

* Going.

be raank wi' dissenters awe oop an' doon, bet that isn't what I's coomd ta esk ya. Awe t' fooaks keen er taakin ye to-morn, an' Mees Minna, t' bonny Mees Minna, as wed wi' thee—a canna spak' er as owt else—oop t' Raise, ta t' gap——."

" I do not quite understand, Job, what they would have us do."

" Why, it's joost this, Mr. Melchior, they's fit ta greet at loss er ye, an' t' conny lady, an' they'd like ta taak ye oop t' Raise, an' nit t' nags."

" They want to pull us up the Raise, and take out the horses. Tell them, Job, from me, that they shall, if they wish, and thank them, and here is something for them to drink our health with ; but I must hear of no one getting too much."

" Nae, nae, Meester Melchior, I'll promus ye, we'll nin er oos be gettin' beered oop. I'll warrn oos it sall be ni meear than a lile tinny soop, nit enoo ta mecak a toteler flaayed."*

The next day, by noon, the Abbey was

* Frightened.

surrounded.   Every man, woman, and child,
in Black Moss, had come up there.   The
halt and the blind had found those to lead
them to where they could hear the vicar's
voice, for he was yet the vicar to them ; and
by fifty stout statesmen and shepherds was
Guy Melchior and his wife taken up the
Raise.

Nothing quite like to it in Black Moss
had been ever seen before ; and there has
been nothing at all like to it from that day
until now.   The only check that came to
the perfect fulfilment of the dean's happiness,
as he looked around upon the people he had
loved so well, was that he had to leave behind so great a gathering of faithful hearts.

At last they stood still in the beginning
of the Gap, and the horses took the place of
that loyal human team.   Then the multitude drew round, every man and woman
pressing forward to catch some sound at
parting, until presently a shout went up
that "t'aald vicar had summut ta spak."

"Bet he's evven meear than t'vicar noo,
Job ; he's a serious deal girter—th' dean's

a terble girt mon, he is, hawivver," said
Sawrey Knotts, who, as the sexton, was the
recognised expounder of all ecclesiastical
titles and distinctions in the place.

"Hod thy din, Jimmy," said the swiller
to a young man who, by his voice and
pantomime about the carriage door showed
that his sorrowing was very strong—"t'vicar
canna tauk for thy serious clatter. I'll put
thy neb at poak,* thee is like a gae feater,†
mon."

And then the dean got up and looked
upon the upturned faces which were waiting
for his words, and said, as he struggled to
stay the trembling of his voice—"God bless
you all my good, true friends. We shall
never forget this day——"

"No, we never shall," echoed the little
voice by his side, and the little voice was
almost drowned in a sob.

"Think of us, and when you pray do not
let us drop out of your prayers;" and then
fearing lest he should quite break down, if

* Bag or sack.   † Dancer.

he tried further to speak to them, he gave the word to drive on.

"Nae, nae, Meester Melchior," pleaded a woman, coming to the front and holding up her little one for the dean to take into his arms, "nit till th' lady hae kist t'bairn— spak summut ta t' goode Lord for th' lile yan."

And so it came to pass that Guy Melchior had to take all the children in his arms before the mothers were appeased, and certain of them would have their babies also taken up by Sybil.

Job Redcar, the while, had fairly given way, and he was bowed down wailing at the back of the carriage, and he crept round clutching the dean's hand, and crying out, "I's maisliken,* a knaa varra, bet ya's sick a terble cheerful loovin' parson ya meeak'd es awe ta dae guide ; there's nowt shapt† like ya left at coontry. I canna bide t' thowt er lossin ya, I canna that."

"I go away hoping we all may meet again, Job," said the dean, seeking to com-

* Foolish. † Shaped, or fashioned.

fort the sorrowing swiller, whilst Job himself first squeezed the hand of Guy, and then of Sybil, "if not here, hereafter. I pray God that there I may see you all, all that I have even known since first I came amongst you."

"Ay, ay, Meester‘Melchior, bet Gideon Cuyp a wud nit like sooa weel ta meet he yonder; er I shud be geean'd doon; itwud be trailin' ma thru hell. I shud feel terble oogly agin him, a shud, hawivver," said Redcar; but no one heard him but the dean.

And then cheer upon cheer went up as they were driven through the Gap, some stragglers the while hanging on to get a last grasp of "t' aald vicar's kneaf;"* for notwithstanding all that Sawrey Knotts had said about the dignity and office of a dean, Guy Melchior was to them the vicar still.

"And noo, me lads," screamed Job, "a cheer an' a girt cheer for their lile yans; they'll mappen hae deal er childers; ameeast† awe t' parsons dae."

"Ay barn, Job, yere for ivver reet; she looked seek as a peat joost noo," said an old

---

* Fist.   † Almost.

woman who spoke on this matter as one who might speak with some authority. "There be yan* coomin' likely."

And as the cheers rang out, the people filled and surged in the beginning of the Gap, to look on the last of those who were leaving them.

"See their dear faces there, Guy," proudly whispered Sybil to her husband, "how every one loves you!"

The heart of Guy Melchior was very full. "Darling," he murmured, as she nestled to his side, "there is no void here now."

For was not Sybil standing in the Gap?

* One.

THE END.

www.ingramcontent.com/pod-product-compliance
Lightning Source LLC
Chambersburg PA
CBHW060521030726
47498CB00004B/1023